Into the Ruins

Issue 4

Winter 2017

Published February 2017 by Figuration Press
Portland, Oregon

Into the Ruins is a project and publication of Figuration Press,
a small publication house focused on alternate visions of the future
and alternate ways of understanding the world,
particularly in ecological contexts.

intotheruins.com

figurationpress.com

ISBN 13: 978-0-9978656-2-2
ISBN 10: 0-9978656-2-8

Editor's Note:
One year in, I am deeply gratified and in many ways astounded
by the incredible support shown for this project.
THANK YOU TO EVERYONE WHO HAS SUPPORTED INTO THE RUINS.
I look forward to a second year—and perhaps spin-off projects, as well.
On that note, please don't forget to renew your subscription if you haven't already;
turn to the final page for details and instructions.

Comments and feedback always welcome at editor@intotheruins.com
Comments for authors will be forwarded.

Issue 4
Winter 2017

TABLE OF CONTENTS

PREAMBLE

STORIES

REVIEWS

PREAMBLE

FINDING NEW PATHS

BY JOEL CARIS

As I settle into the role of editor, I more and more realize that one of the complexities of this job is in deciding what kinds of futures are feasible and what kinds aren't. It's an odd task to have, not least of all because I'm hardly the most qualified to take on this role; there are plenty of people far smarter and more studied than I am who might better parse the likely future we all face. But more to the point, trying to figure out what types of futures are feasible strikes me as a fool's errand. The future is not only far too messy, uncertain, and complex to easily figure that out, but the worldview and imaginative constraints placed upon all of us by our own culture severely limits our ability to anticipate what may happen in the future, simply because the future is inevitably going to feature a whole host of cultures utterly unlike our own. In their difference, they will be capable of imagining and pursuing courses of thought, study, technology, politics, social organization, economics, and so much more that simply does not occur—and often feels impossible—to those of us living in this particular culture during this particular time. Much as our particular culture has pursued new modes of living that would have seemed impossible to far different cultures of the past, the future cultures still yet to sprout will inevitably find ways of living that are largely inconceivable to us today.

Of course, it's not just this culture that places limits on the type of future we can imagine, but our own individual thoughts, viewpoints, and preferences that do, as well. For instance, thanks to my own intense interest and past experience in sustainable agriculture, I readily respond to stories set within future agricultural societies making use of organic growing techniques and organized in small villages or modest towns. I'm confident that such a future is both feasible and likely, not only due to my own knowledge and experience, but because such organizing principles have worked in the past when fossil fuels and industrialization were far less common or largely absent from the landscape. That does not change the fact, though, that such portrayals of the future resonate with me at a personal level as well as at my own particular level of knowledge and understanding. It's just as possible that other portrayals of the future might strike me as uninteresting or lacking in intrigue due to my personal tastes, or as doubtful and unlikely due not to their inherent ability to be created in the future, but due to my own limited knowledge and understanding of certain types of technology, social organization, economic feasibility, and so on.

Even simple personal bias can play a role here. For instance, I loathe the idea of a landscape littered with self-driving cars, despite the fact that every major car manufacturer, a good number of tech companies, and plenty of others factions are all piling into this particular form of technology as the fetish du jour. While the self-driving car fad has the clear makings of a bubble, that doesn't mean that the technology and its use won't become somewhat common in the decades ahead, if it can outrun the steady depletion of fossil fuels, economic upheaval, political chaos, common sense, and all the other challenges creating a headwind for the technology. It may well be that fifteen or twenty years from now, self-driving vehicles are common enough on our roads, pushed by social narrative, economic benefit to large corporations and investors, politics of convenience, and the declining feasibility of owning a personal automobile. I hope that isn't the case—and if they do become common, I don't expect them to last long in the coming chaos of our times—but I can't rule out the possibility, either. (I'm still convinced flying cars are never happening, though; don't expect to see a story featuring them in *Into the Ruins* any time soon.)

Personal bias can come through in the types of stories selected, too. As anyone who has followed this journal for its first year has likely figured out by now, I've been raised on a steady diet of literary fiction, though with a good smattering of genre fiction to go with that. Despite this being ostensibly a genre publication, I don't shy away from stories that delve deep into personal relationships and echo more as literary fiction. My own contribution to this issue, "An Expected Chill," features just such a focus. However, I enjoy a well-written and action-oriented piece, as well, such as Ralph Walker's included story, "The Toxicity of Water." In fact, one focus I have for future issues is attempting to bring in more writing that feels like genre fiction while maintaining a level of quality that I demand for inclusion in *Into the Ruins*. It's a tricky tightrope to walk, and I realize that it's made trickier by my own preferences and predilections. My stalwart Associate Editor, Shane Wilson, helps to give me another perspective, but I still take it upon myself to make the final decisions.

Some of those decisions can be a challenge, with the reason why going back to what I wrote above: the question of what kind of futures are feasible within future resource and energy constraints is so very influenced by the culture within which humans are working. For instance, what kind of technologies can we expect to be workable and widespread a thousand years from now? That's an incredibly challenging question to answer. Again, I would place organic agriculture as a very likely, feasible, and widely-used technology, but even that is not absolutely a guarantee. And when we extend out beyond food, the question becomes even more a challenge. Solar hot water heaters, low-tech wind and water turbines, animal and human labor all seem quite likely to me, as does passive solar design, mycoremediation, canal transportation, and sailing for specialized global trade. But what about, say, the cross-species communication technology found in Chloe Woods' story, "Blackfin"? Is that feasible? If so, how likely is it to look the way it looks in her story? These are challenging and at least somewhat unanswerable questions that go back to at least one of the guidelines for submissions: "They should obey natural laws as we currently understand them." That's a surprisingly complicated guideline, in particular due to those last five words. In the case of "Blackfin," it could bring us back to questions of what kind of language and culture other species have, what kind of self-aware-ness they possess, and if, assuming they do have language and self-awareness, we could find a way to bridge the gap between species and literally speak with them—or if we could, what such a culture that accomplished that goal might look like.

To my mind, nothing portrayed in "Blackfin" is an impossibility. We can conduct basic communication with apes, we know dolphins and whales use language to some degree—though there are debates as to the degree it can be called "language"—and in general, we seem to be growing ever more aware of the complexity of plant and animal intelligence. From a personal perspective (here we go again) I am very sympathetic to the idea that other species on this planet—both animal and plant—are far more "intelligent" than we have tended to give them credit for. I am also very sympathetic to the idea the world is far more complex and mysterious than our culture tends to believe. And finally, one of my key goals with *Into the Ruins* and Figuration Press in general is to bring to the public more stories that engage our world in a more holistic, ecological, and respectful manner; and bringing in a future in which we are in much more direct communication with other species is one way to do that. Considering that I find it unconvincing that anything in the portrayal of this communication in "Blackfin" is clearly an impossibility (the form of the technology used to conduct the communication provides my biggest misgiving), I tipped toward publishing the story. It didn't hurt, of course, that it is a fine story in its own right, both well-written and compelling in its story and characters.

Finally, the other danger that I want to avoid in my selection of stories is limiting too greatly the possibilities of the future. This, of course, is one of the chief criticisms of the common tropes in science fiction today: that it too often is rooted in glossy futures dominated by space travel and technology that looks and behaves suspiciously like the computer technology of today, as though the way we live our lives now is the only way we might live them in the future. This poses a danger not only in the way we are able to imagine living, but in the continuation of the ecological cost and destruction that comes with the modes of living we employ today. We desperately need to imagine different types of futures so as to broaden the possibilities before us. That not only opens the door to better ways of living in terms of the ecological world, but it also leads to the possibilities of more interesting, creative, and humane ways of living that could lead to greater happiness and satisfaction. (And yes, I realize that has the whiff of "myth of progress" to it, but I certainly believe there are more satisfying ways of organizing our culture and society than the ones we most use today, and see no reason we can't discover those with a bit of hard work.)

Without imagining different social organizations, different political structures, different economic principles, and different forms of technology, we are doomed to continue down the same failed paths, beating our heads against the wall of diminishing and negative returns. There are a thousand other paths still available to us, which we have hardly explored, that might lead to fascinating futures of a different type. It's extremely hard to imagine those futures in the limiting confines of our current culture, but I believe that's one of the most pressing tasks in front of us, and it's one of the driving purposes behind this magazine. In service of that effort, I intend to continue to reach for stories that I believe are both feasible and unique, and to question deeply doubts I have about a story to determine if those doubts stem from hard natural limits—good reason not to publish a story, so far as I'm concerned—or simply the function of intellectual limitation imposed by our current culture. And even as I make these decisions, I ask that readers hold my feet—and the feet of the authors published within—to the fire by writing to us, debating the futures portrayed, pointing out flaws and confirming possibilities, refining proposed technologies or modes of living, and just generally coming along with us on this journey and pointing us, indefatigably, toward all the paths that we keep missing. This publication is a project, after all, to imagine new ways of living. It's a fun project, to be sure—not a trudge of finger-pointing, but hopefully instead a thoughtful and considered celebration of possibility—but its strength will ultimately not come through my particular opinion and personal point of view, but through the collective efforts of contributing writers and readers, all of us working to conceive of all the possible futures that our broader society at large has decided aren't worth pursuing or are incapable of being enacted. With every passing day, it seems we need these new futures more and more. I hope that within these pages, we can collaboratively discover them.

— *Portland, Oregon*
February 27, 2017

Into the Ruins is published quarterly by Figuration Press. We publish deindustrial science fiction that explores a future defined by natural limits, energy and resource depletion, industrial decline, climate change, and other consequences stemming from the reckless and shortsighted exploitation of our planet, as well as the ways that humans will adapt, survive, live, die, and thrive within this future.

One year, four issue subscriptions to *Into the Ruins* are $39. You can subscribe by visiting intotheruins.com/subscribe or by mailing a check made out to Figuration Press to:

Figuration Press / 3515 SE Clinton Street / Portland, OR 97202

To submit your work for publication, please visit intotheruins.com/submissions or email submissions@intotheruins.com.

All issues of *Into the Ruins* are printed on paper, first and foremost. Electronic versions will be made available as high quality PDF downloads. Please visit our website for more information. The opinions expressed by the authors do not necessarily reflect the opinions of Figuration Press or *Into the Ruins*. Except those expressed by Joel Caris, since this is a sole proprietorship. That said, all opinions are subject to (and commonly do) change, for despite the Editor's occasional actions suggesting the contrary, it turns out he does not know everything and the world often still surprises him.

EDITOR-IN-CHIEF
JOEL CARIS

ASSOCIATE EDITOR
SHANE WILSON

DESIGNER
JOEL CARIS

WITH THANKS TO
SHANE WILSON
JOHN MICHAEL GREER
OUR SUBSCRIBERS

SPECIAL THANKS TO
KATE O'NEILL

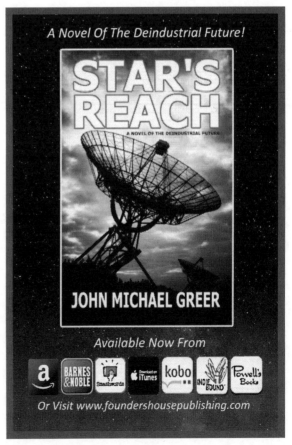

CONTRIBUTORS

CHLOE WOODS hails from the beautiful but damp city of Edinburgh, Scotland. She is in the middle of a Master's degree in Human Evolution and Behaviour, which combines her love of obscure topics that shouldn't be obscure and questions nobody can answer. She is also a trad fiddle player, a bird-watcher and an avid befriender of cats, and she has been working on the same piece of knitting for three years. Chloe is in her early twenties and she would like to be a writer when she grows up.

W. JACK SAVAGE is a retired broadcaster and educator. He is the author of seven books, including *Imagination: The Art of W. Jack Savage* (wjacksavage.com). To date, more than fifty of Jack's short stories and over seven hundred of his paintings and drawings have been published worldwide. Jack and his wife Kathy live in Monrovia, California. Jack is, as usual, responsible for this issue's cover art.

JOEL CARIS is a gardener and homesteader, occasional farmer, passionate advocate for local and community food systems, sporadic writer, voracious reader, sometimes prone to distraction and too attendant to detail, a little bit crazy, a cynical optimist, and both deeply empathetic toward and frustrated with humanity. He is your friendly local editor and publisher. As a reader of this journal and perhaps other writings of his, he hopes you don't too easily tire of his voice and perspective. He lives in Oregon with an amazing, endlessly patient woman who somehow makes him a better person every single damn day.

WILSON BERTRAM was born in Ireland, brought up and lived in Kenya, South Africa and England. He worked as an auditor. He is interested in history, and feels he has been living through it, having seen two countries begin the slide away from civilisation and now experiencing it in a third.

Born in the gritty Navy town of Bremerton, Washington and raised in the south Seattle suburbs, JOHN MICHAEL GREER started writing about as soon as he could hold a pencil. He is the author of more than forty nonfiction books and four novels, including the deindustrial novel *Star's Reach*, as well as the weekly blog "The Archdruid Report," and has edited four volumes of the *After Oil* series of deindustrial science fiction anthologies. These days he lives in Cumberland, Maryland, an old red brick mill town in the north central Appalachians, with his wife Sara.

RALPH WALKER is an architect and writer in New Jersey. His work, both built and on the page, explores our rapidly changing environment. A graduate of Syracuse University, Ralph has been practicing architecture on both coasts for twenty years. His science fiction previously received an Honorable Mention from the Writers of the Future contest. He is currently working on his debut novel. He can be found on twitter at @RW_Igloo or his website, located at ralphwalkerauthor.com

At 62 years of age, JEANNE LABONTE is a lifelong resident of northern New Hampshire. Her day job is with a small mail order business (to pay the bills) but her main interests are writing, drawing, gardening, reading and publishing personal observations about them, as well as about the beauty of the local environment, in her blog New Hampshire Green Leaves, located at jeannemlabonte.com

JASON HEPPENSTALL is an ex-journalist, newspaper editor and energy analyst from the English Midlands. After spending years travelling around the world and living in Denmark and Spain he now resides with his family in Cornwall, UK, where he sustainably manages a damp woodland and grows mushrooms. Describing himself as an optimistic realist, Jason writes about facing up to our future on his blog, *22 Billion Energy Slaves*, and released a book in 2015 called *The Path to Odin's Lake* about the spiritual aspect of the Long Descent.

LETTERS TO THE EDITOR

Editor's Note: On January 8th, I posted a blog entry on the Into the Ruins *website asking readers what they planned to do in the new year to help mitigate the impact of decline and consequence taking place around us. The following three letters are responses to that query. The remaining letters stand on their own.*

Dear Editor,

One of the possible responses to the crises of our time available for individual application is philosophy. The issues that face humanity are large. The issues that face individuals are often difficult. I find that having a practical philosophy tucked in my pocket is a sure source of strength in times of stress. In particular the Stoic school of thought holds much appeal. The basic idea of Stoicism could be summarized as the pursuit of virtue, or excellence, based on living in harmony with nature. Stoic philosophy puts action and behavior ahead of thought and emotion, because they believed emotions caused destructive errors in judgement due to the interplay between divine Reason or Fate, and human Free Will. As such, Stoic training aims at helping individuals achieve a joy that arises from fortitude, self-control and being virtuous rather than from the pursuit of pleasure.

For those interested in learning and applying Stoicism in their lives, nothing beats going to the sources and reading some of the great translations (or originals if you can) of Epictetus, Seneca, Marcus Aurelius and the others. There are also a number of recent books (within the last ten years) that have embraced Stoic principles. It is my duty as a library guy to list a few of them here for others who might be interested. *A Guide to the Good Life: The Ancient Art of Stoic Joy* by William Irvine is the best accessible guide to start with in my opinion. It has a concise history of the philosophic school, an overview of their basic psychological techniques and some Stoic advice as well as thoughts on how to use the philosophy in modern life. Though professor Irvine is an academic at the University of Dayton his book is not at all stodgy and is a real pleasure in prose. (Which is great because many of the other books that give an overview and history of this subject are from highfalutin academics who make it hard to extract anything practical from their cramped pages.)

Next up is the much touted tome by Nassim Nicholas Taleb, *Antifragile: Things That Gain from Disorder*. Taleb's book is like a free range chicken: it finds sustenance from all manner of topics. As such, Stoicism isn't the main subject, but enough of it is littered throughout the book that it warrants inclusion. Also it is a damn entertaining and thought-provoking book on many levels. What I like best from it, as pertains to the present discussion, is his idea of "Post Traumatic Growth." It seems that Post Traumatic Stress Disorder is all over the place these days, but Nicholas is brave enough to remind us of all the growth that also occurs when a person or society is confronted with painful experiences. This is something that doesn't see enough discussion or application.

The third book on my list comes from Navy SEAL Eric Greitens. Books by Navy SEALS seem to be real popular of late. Maybe it's because Americans are used to living a soft life full of entertainment saturation, and those who have gone through the elite training of U.S. Special Forces represent a kind of hardihood many of us would like to revive. His book *Resilience: Hard Won Wisdom for Living a Better Life* is worth reading twice. He seems to have a natural take on Taleb's idea of Post Traumatic Growth as it is addressed as a series of letters to a fellow SEAL suffering from PTSD. In each of the chapters he invites his reader to look at such fun subjects as pain, responsibility, and death. He draws on the Stoics quite a bit. My favorite idea from this book is that feelings and thoughts should not be the basis of action, but rather right (virtuous) action produces good thoughts and feelings, a reversal of the accepted "wisdom" that seems to be so common today. For me it is

easy to not want to do things because I don't feel like it, but when I place action ahead of feeling I often find a pleasant satisfaction to be my reward. And that helps me remember that passing emotions need not dictate my behavior.

Two other titles deserve mentioning, though I haven't gotten around to them yet myself. *The Obstacle is the Way: the Timeless Art of Turning Trials into Triumph*, and *The Daily Stoic: 366 Meditations on Wisdom, Perseverance, and the Art of Living*, both by Ryan Holiday. I hope to get to them over the next few months. There are probably many other new books out there tapping into the wisdom of the ancients that I haven't heard of but these are some that are adding to my own life and helping create what I think of as a quiet Stoic revival. All are great antidotes to unruly habits of thought.

I'll leave with this quote from Epictetus: "You must know it is no easy thing for a principle to become a man's own, unless each day he maintain it and hear it maintained, as well as work it out in his own life."

Kind regards,

Justin Patrick Moore
Cincinnati, Ohio

Dear Editor,

Happy New Year and thanks for the invitation to share.

My partner and I are gathering

with a group of friends, all of whom live within walking distance, to discuss philosophy and strategy and prepare for collapse. As a starting point, we're reading and discussing the book *Prosper* by Chris Martenson and Adam Taggart, using the book as a guide for our joint resiliency efforts. Although we're not going into the "bunker mentality," it certainly seems like the right time to begin getting some supplies and support together for likely hard times ahead. Really need to hop to it and get food and water in place before the inauguration.

Up to this point in my career, I've been mostly a hospital pharmacist. I'm beginning to turn my almost-retirement-career toward public health, starting a course in integrative health (i.e. low-tech preventive medicine supplanting high-tech interventional medicine whenever possible) and have also just signed up to be a volunteer for the Medical Reserve Corps. New skills I'm developing are darning socks for the first time, attempting to repair small appliances and thinking about pressure canning. It's become sobering to realize that all of that stuff in the basement that's been lingering there for years is now taking up valuable space that can be used for food, water or shelter, so it's going out.

It's most interesting to explore the balance between preparing for hard times and enjoying current good times. I don't want to become known as the doom and gloom person in my circle of friends, yet I think those who

say preparing is fatalistic and futile are consciously in denial about how delicate is the technology (and the politics!) that makes our convenient and comfortable lives possible.

Amy Kennedy
Pittsburgh, Pennsylvania

Dear Editor,

I have the same New Year's resolution as last year, and that's to quit smoking . . . again. I know this will help the environment, but that's not really why I'm doing it. I hope to help the environment as much as I can in 2017, but not through a single resolution. Instead, I have a series of goals. They all revolve around a common theme, and that is food. We currently use ten calories of fossil fuels to generate each calorie of food, and that's unacceptable. I live in a suburban environment on the edge of a rural area, so I know I can do better than that!

First I will finish construction of my greenhouse, hopefully in time for starting seeds (but if not, I can start them in the house like I usually do). Next I want to start raising meat rabbits. This is a bigger challenge because my construction skills are limited, and I'm starting from knowing basically nothing about rabbits. If the rabbits work out, next will be quail. If they don't I will skip the quail this year and wait until next year. Either way, I'll be contacting my beekeeping friend to hopefully start a hive. I don't know the time of year you start a new hive, so I might just spend this year acquiring equipment to use next year.

Finally, I will intensify my efforts to live off the wild land base. This means more fishing (oh, darn) and more time learning to forage wild plants. A surprising number of people around here already forage, they just don't call it that. They eat wild raspberries and pick wild asparagus, and they gather mulberries and hickory nuts, but if you tell them you are going foraging they say "You're going to poison yourself!" which entertains me to no end! If all goes well, I might try ice fishing next winter . . . maybe. I'm a baby about the cold!

I hope everyone reading meets their goals and I hope that the journey is more rewarding than you all dreamed possible (even if you hit the occasional snag). Let's have a great 2017!

Sincerely,

Jessi Thompson
Spring Grove, Illinois

Dear Editor,

It is astounding how so much data can produce so little information.

All I wanted to know was: How many North Carolina townships were flooded during the week-long Hurricane Matthew event?

You would think that so simple, so quantifiable, so verifiable and POLITICALLY IMPORTANT a question would be answered with ease and dispatch on any of a number of internet sources with some pretension to quality and authority. A government site, a research arm in a university, a TV news or actual newspaper. You would be quite wrong in supposing this, as I was.

I never expected much help from Google, which has been optimized to the point of uselessness; it has become a mere conveyor belt of merchandising for the highest bidder from the least informed. But how could I have known that ALL the factual matter that used to be available in newspapers (to wit, summaries, graphs, and charts of verified, carefully digested, duly processed data distilled into USEFUL information) was entirely absent from the much touted and endlessly self-glorified Information Highway? Information low-road is more like it. And washed out to boot.

By scraping around a whole lot of over-animated "interactive" sites—heavily larded with nine-color pretty-pretty images and aerial photos, hence, expensive to me in terms of used-up bandwidth of which I have little enough to spare—I finally discovered that approximately thirty counties out of North Carolina's one hundred were most heavily watered. But an actual real-live TEXT LIST of those counties together with a TEXT-LIST of the flooded townships within those counties—pffffft! Nothing. Nada. Zero to the max, man.

If there had been such a list, shoot, great-gums and spitfire, I could have counted them on my own ten-digit, hand-held computing aid. My curiosity would have been satisfied (for the moment) and I had been no further trouble to anyone. Until I started asking for a similar list of farms and private wells so affected. But the one is as invisible to ordinary citizens as the other: a huge glob, an undigested bolus of data+pictures is out there on the Web, but the Truth is not in it.

That something so simple, so basic to the workings of a real democracy as a map of the town-level political units affected by a climate change-related weather event is not readily available to the citizens of this state, is a clear marker of the degradation of the Fourth Estate and probably a deliberate policy on the part of corporate-corrupted news media. I bet if you had the bucks to belong to some corporate crony-club in the urban power centers, that such detailed, instantly graspable information would be at your manicured fingertips. Because there might be money in it, see? Municipal bonds sales, or water privateers, seeking whose public utilities they might next devour.

But a numbered list of actual names of all the towns half drowned . . . uh unh. No sirree bob.

Can't let the facts out of the moneybag, now can we?

G. Kay Bishop
Durham, North Carolina

Dear Editor,

We can postulate and intellectualize collapse, but when people start dying in high numbers, there's no way to prepare for that in advance.

I did want to point out some of us have been experiencing loss for a very long time already. I have heard a few voices in the environmental movement, perplexed by a new environmentalism, where wind farms and solar farms are always good things, no matter where they are placed. I figured it out. The new environmentalism is the urban environmentalism. As all the wilderness has been eaten up by "progress," fewer people ever even saw wilderness in their entire lives. I can tell you, walking on the paved path of a little park in the suburbs is not wilderness, no matter how many pruned, disease-controlled, and fire-managed trees there are. Standing in a pasture in a deeply rural area is not wilderness, but it's a little closer. Those of us who have seen truly wild places and fell in love have been watching the systematic torture and destruction of the wild for a very long time. No matter what happens, I will find joy in the blades of grass breaking through the old sidewalks and the trees growing through the walls of what used to be buildings. I can't guarantee I will live long enough to watch decay and renewal outpace bulldozers and destruction, but I really want to.

If you deeply fear what is coming, go outside and walk. Look at the plants and animals. They even live in cities, but they are small and hard to find. Look at the birds. Look at the life. Maybe you will recognize it for what it is when you see it growing back, the resilience, the determination to survive, the triumphs and tragedies that happen every day, the spider and the butterfly. I saw footage of penguins surfing huge waves to be smashed up onto cliffs twenty feet high. They kept smashing into the jagged rocks and falling back into the rough sea to try again, smashing up into the cliffs again and again until they finally reached the top, to the only place in the world where they lay their eggs. I saw that and said, "There's an animal determined to live! The entire species evolved to do THAT!"

As a culture, we collectively have no idea what we've lost, what the cost was of all this progress. The last people who remember grew up at the very edges of the rural areas, looking outward onto vast reaches of wild and dangerous land and water. These last people are all heartbroken. They watch more and more beauty ripped apart as mountain-tops are removed to mine coal and forests are clearcut for every imaginable wood and paper product, and even the ocean is choked to clogging with plastic. With decline, all of this recedes. The best thing we can possibly do for our ecosystem is leave it alone. Slowly, life will come back and new species will fill niches left by the old, but even before then, the wilds will encroach on everything we leave behind. Look for that, look for the easing of our collect-ive land-use footprints as abandoned shopping malls collapse and their parking lots grow grass again. There will be many moments of astonishment and opportunities for joy, even amidst the loss. Look for it, for as our hubris is washed away by forces of nature, wild and rugged beauty will return. Don't give up hope yet, for the next epoch's tigers and woolly mammoths have not yet been born. If you are looking for the signs of collapse around you, keep an eye out for the corresponding signs of re-newal and regeneration. If you learn to see it, it will feed your soul in a way in-dustrial civilization never could.

Sincerely,

Jessi Thompson
Spring Grove, Illinois
(Reprinted from The Archdruid Report comment section with permission.)

Into the Ruins *welcomes letters to the editor from our readers. We encourage thoughtful commentary on the contents of this issue, the themes of the maga-zine, and humanity's collective future. Readers may email their letters to editor@intotheruins.com or mail to:*

Figuration Press
3515 SE Clinton Street
Portland, OR 97202

Please include your full name, city and state, and an email or phone number. Only your name and location will be printed with any accepted letter.

STORIES

Blackfin

by Chloe Woods

SUNLIGHT GLANCED OFF THE WATER. The sea's surface went rippling from the paddle as it dipped with barely a splash and arced out again to cut across the softly lapping waves; they seemed to swallow sound and slow motion, distorting everything below. The knotted wood glistened for a moment and vanished again, reappeared, disappeared, and in this hypnotic pattern the narrow kayak cut smoothly across and away from the entrance to the fjord. The hills and the buildings of the Karvag Atlantic Institute receded into the distance. Shimmering ocean stretched out to the horizon. High above, the summer sun burned.

Tasker felt his eyes burning too, from the sting of salt and glare of light on the waves. He tried not to think about the narrowness of the boat, bobbing about in the endless water, or the depth of the sea below its hull, or—

Well done, he chided himself. Did you think that was going to work?

Someone had once told him that fear of deep water was an odd sort of trait in a marine biologist. Tasker had retorted that it was respect, not fear—and in this case the problem was less the water than the boat. Now, Tasker had nothing against boats, which was to say he had nothing against proper boats: the barges on the canals back home, or the great triple-masted clinkers that sailed out in the channel, or even the smaller fishing vessel he'd bargained for a ride on from Bergen. They were all fine. But this, in Tasker's opinion, was not a boat. It was a floating tree with paddles.

He knew better than to say this out loud. He might have only met Mella Karlsdotter three days ago, but he'd learned quickly not to insult her kayak. Tasker decided against making any comment at all. All the same, when Mella balanced the double-ended paddle on her knees and let the kayak slow to a drift, she turned to shush him.

"I wasn't—" said Tasker, and shut up.

The water lapped against the sides of their small vessel and the ripples faded away into nothing. The sea seemed perfect and unbroken.

Until it wasn't.

A blast of spray broke the surface first, followed by a rising black dorsal fin, folded over at the tip. Tasker couldn't decide if it was larger or smaller than he had expected. Somewhere in his imagination the blackfin were giants of the ocean, big enough to swallow a man whole, bigger than any creature he had ever met—and yet they were smaller than the whale bones and dinosaur bones hung from wire in the Hillerød museum where he had gazed in awe at the wonders of the world from before he could remember. The blackfin were related to dolphins, he recalled, more closely than to the great gone whales, and they were smaller than some of the whales yet remaining. This thought prompted another scrap of information that had until recently been trivia: the females had significantly smaller dorsal fins than the males. Like these.

A second fin appeared, this one with a notch in it. A third, much smaller, bobbed along beside it. Then a third adult. Having broken the surface to breathe, the first ducked underneath again, and the rest followed, their slick black backs folded up by the waves.

"That's Paris," said Mella, under her breath. "The second one is Wick, and her baby. And that's Sundsvall."

"You can tell?" said Tasker. He couldn't tell if her glare meant it was a stupid question or that he'd spoken too loud. The second, he realised a moment later: the following eye-roll was probably Mella's answer to the first. She didn't dignify the question with an actual response. Tasker huffed to himself, thinking it wasn't such a ridiculous thing to ask—how could anybody tell all those creatures apart? There was a book of the local blackfin in the Institute, with details of their ages and family connections and neatly-drawn sketches of their dorsal fins and other identifying features, but though he'd looked at it for two hours yesterday he didn't even recognise the names. Anyway, the blackfin all looked pretty similar to him. Even with the book on his lap—not that he'd have got it anywhere near the water before Doctor Ebbeson gave him a thrashing for it—Tasker doubted he could have begun to identify them.

Mella, though, had been working with them her whole life. So maybe it was stupid to ask.

The blackfin rose to the surface again, closer to the boat, and cruised in. Mella took a couple of short strokes with the paddle. The first of the blackfin ducked before cutting across to lazily breach the surface right in front of their path, with another blast of spray that splattered over them.

"Hi to you too," said Mella, with a wave to Tasker. He jumped to attention to sort through the piles of kit packed around and over his legs and behind Mella's seat, unclip a couple of boxes, screw several things together and finally plug in the battery and drop the line into the water. Mella took the waterproofed screen while Tasker continued to reel out the line. The camera sank into the water. As it did so it began to pick up images of the blackfin, blurry and massive in the water. A shoal of silver fish darted into the depths.

"Watch this," said Mella. "Oh, youse hush-hush be," she added, in a fond tone that meant it obviously wasn't intended for her human companion. She flicked a couple of switches, and the deep blue-greys of the image became a series of rippling lines marked in glowing red and pink. Tasker leaned forward as best he could to watch the screen over her shoulders.

"Wow . . ."

He knew what the images were. He'd seen them before—in travelling exhibits at the museum, then many times at the Universities of Gothenburg and København, and most recently during his induction at the Institute—but always at a remove: recorded, and far away. He'd never sat in a bobbing scrap of wood while the camera sent back echofilm from water only ten metres from his toes.

This was what the blackfin saw.

It was the closest a human would get, at any rate, excepting those blind people who'd also learned to bounce sound off objects to navigate a dark world. A human could only think of seeing sound: maybe the blackfin had a concept of hearing images. They were much more adept.

One of them swung lazily towards the camera, lunged for it with a gaping maw, and at the last moment ducked away. Mella giggled. The other blackfin were drifting about fifty or so paces from the kayak. Tasker wondered what they thought of this one's playful behaviour: indulgent amusement, or embarrassment, or impatience because they wanted to be somewhere else? He would have struggled to read the mood of a human group at this distance, far less that of members of another species. Exasperation? Pride? Jealousy at the boldness—no. If Tasker could remember anything of what he'd been told about Mella's relationship with the blackfin, it was that none of them were shy of her. Not from the pod that lived at the mouth of the Institute's fjord. If the blackfin had a folk memory of long-ago ancestors who'd been hunted or held in tiny, cramped pools until they died of heartbreak, they were also smart enough to know that not all humans were the same.

He'd already forgotten which of the blackfin this one was, and he didn't dare ask again. He stayed quiet while the great creature playfully carried out more mock-attacks on the camera. Mella kept up a stream of babbling conversation that Tasker understood little of, and not only because he could only hear one half of it and knew few of the individuals involved. Most of the words were Nordic (though a few were from the unfamiliar Romsdal dialect, which didn't help; and Tasker wasn't a Nordic native himself), but the way she strung them into sentences was like nothing he'd ever heard before. Tasker did manage to catch the name she addressed the blackfin by: Sundsvall. He repeated it to himself while Sundsvall launched one more attack on the camera and this time hit it lightly in passing, sending the images on the screen whirling, then settled in beside the boat.

"Tat aright-aright being. I bringing have somebody meet youse. Tat's meaning noes, I sorry-sorry being, I not tisday can be coming water-walk." The blackfin snorted water over the side of the boat. By now it was beginning to seep into Tasker's clothes. Proper waterproofing was for equipment, not for people, who would dry out quickly enough on a warm day. He wiped the liquid from his face and tried to decide if he should think of it as seawater or blackfin mucus while Mella continued. "He researcher being. Youse be wanting-waiting talk him?"

The other blackfin were starting to drift closer to the kayak. Something made Mella laugh. She made another comment, then from the pile of kit pulled out an earpiece, played around with the settings and handed it to Tasker. "Sundsvall wants to say hello. Tis researcher being, Sundsvall. He not being knowing how talk inproper. Be-youse nice tat's meaning, good-good?"

Tasker clipped the earpiece on. His ear was filled with a rushing sound like the soughing of waves breaking on the beach, and his first wild thought was that this was the sound of the sea; then almost immediately he wanted to scold himself for the mistake. It wasn't the sea. It was the slow in-and-out of Sundsvall's breathing.

Her voice sounded so close it made him jump, but the human words were more startling still, even though he'd known they were coming. Not even Mella could understand the melodic natural speech of the blackfin. It didn't help that the voice had the same clipped accent as a weather vane, tech-generated rather than natural, and to Tasker's ear sounded even more garbled than Mella's speech.

"Greetings be day good-good researcher youse."

"Um—hello, Sunds—may I call you Sundsvall?"

"Yesses, researcher youse. Youse yesses own-name my may being using of."

"Right, well, my name is—it's not 'researcher,' it's . . . it's Tasker." Trailing off, Tasker felt his cheeks flush red. Could the translator even process a name? Apparently he wasn't any better at introducing himself to blackfin than people.

He scowled at Mella, who was valiantly trying not to laugh.

Sundsvall didn't even try.

Tasker would never like kayaks. Mella tried to teach him to paddle, about a week later, close enough to the shore that the water came up to Tasker's waist when he fell in. Spitting out salt water, he watched as Mella glided over with easy strokes

Tasker couldn't muster up the will to be jealous of. He wanted a real boat—a boat that wouldn't capsize again when he tried to climb back into it, as Mella insisted he learn to do, since he would need to be able to re-kayak himself if he wanted to go swimming with the blackfin. And that he would need to do if he wanted to get anything done.

"At least you can swim," said Mella, while they dried themselves off in the boathouse. "We had a woman from Uppsala, not long ago. Big city. She was hopeless in the water."

"One of the linguists?" asked Tasker, amused to think of Uppsala as the big city. Here at the edge of the world, it might seem like it. It was dwarfed by Lyon, the biggest place Tasker had ever visited, half a million souls and counting—though they said some of the sprawling cities on the plains were bigger.

"No, they were all right. This one was an archaeologist. Asked stupid questions."

It was another week before Mella deemed him competent enough to swim from the kayak in deep water. He felt safer in the water, oddly enough, than he did in the kayak—perhaps because you couldn't fall in the water when you were already in it, and at least in part thanks to the reassuring bulk of the blackfin around him, half-lumbering, half-graceful. By then Tasker could tell most of those they'd met apart, though he still sometimes got their names confused, and he'd spoken with several. Curious Sundsvall was almost always there to meet them, often accompanied by her sister and mother, or by a couple of cousins bearing vicious scars from encounters with whalers. (The whaling boats had subsequently had an encounter with Mella's drill and the bottom of the marina. It sounded like their crews had been clever enough to recognise the warning and clear out. Whaling was only a poaching offence, punishable by no more than five years' resettlement, but the local authorities were willing to turn a blind eye to extra-legal retribution. Scorn of the Academy though the Karvag Institute might be, and borderline heretic into the bargain, the people it served were very loyal.)

It was Sundsvall who first agreed to help with the experiments Tasker wanted to run, and it was Sundsvall who edged alongside the kayak on the day he traded the camera for a first-hand view. Tasker might have preferred a blackfin with a less cruel sense of humour for his initiation to the water: Sundsvall found it funny to jump him from behind.

"I can seeing be why youse und Mella are being friends," he said, in his best attempt at the way Mella talked to the blackfin. The radio earpieces were effective enough at transmuting the creatures' speech into something useable by human ears and brains—and even, thanks to the groundbreaking work by Mella's father and great-aunt, recognisable words in human languages—but it would still have been impossible to hold a conversation without concerted translation efforts on both sides. The way the blackfin spoke was different from human speech in a way that went deeper than words and deeper than grammar, and the loss or blurring of non-verbal communication didn't help. Mella was the best because she had learned to talk to the blackfin alongside learning to talk to humans, and even she said it felt a bit like trying to have a conversation in a language she only half-knew. (Mella spoke a fair few human languages, Tasker had learned, with some humiliation. She'd let him mutter under his breath for most of the week before casually mentioning she could understand his Ddansk insults. Hardly anyone spoke Ddansk these days outside the territories of the League cities; and even there Nordic was taking over.)

That was just communication. It didn't even begin to address the ways the blackfin's perspectives on the world were utterly different from those of humans.

It was not simply that colours became shades of grey and up became down. It was not as easy as flipping the categories around. A blackfin's mind was not like that of a human or even of a human in reverse. The hairless monkeys walked on solid earth and breathed the same air they walked in, while the blackfin were torn always between their place in the water and their need to breathe. A human could swim and dive, but a blackfin could not exist on land: they would suffocate under the weight of their own crushed lungs. There were stories about that. All the same, they were drawn to the air and the world above the waves in more than a literal sense. Mella said the younger, curious ones asked incessant questions about this world they would never truly be able to visualise. The sea might be as rich and whole a world as the one on land but water was always in, as clinging as it was supportive, ever changing, ever fluid. The blackfin imagined that humans must feel very exposed to be always in air rather than the safety of water, but that did not mean the deep water held no perils for them. Like birds, the plane of their world was expanded compared to the four cardinal directions; like birds, there were limits. Predators skulked in the depths that even the blackfin feared. One who tried to swim down into the heavy water risked running out of air and drowning. There were stories about that too.

(They had stories. Tasker thought that might be the strongest similarity.)

In some ways they were as intelligent as humans, in some ways more so—but they had no way to grasp materials or make and use tools and so no grasp, cognitively, of the ways they could be used. They had no sense of smell. They had two kinds of sight: one with their eyes, one with their ears. Because they always had to remember to breathe, they never fully slept, and their dreams were rare and fleeting. Those were easier differences to conceptualise but there was always a jolt when Tasker forgot—though every time he was sure he would never forget—and had to be reminded. Talking to them was like walking through a room full of mirrors. They not only shared no culture with humans, but not even the same kind of culture: theirs revolved around the flow of fish and tides, the dulled effects of the seasons, the taste of the water.

Their societies might not be like the human societies of recent times, but here at least there was an echo of something only recently forgotten. The world had always revolved around the need for food, security and sex. The blackfin were only more honest about it than modern humans in their cities and universities. Their lives were most similar to those of hunter-gatherers, and indeed missionaries who'd lived among them were among those who came to make comparisons. The place was usually a relief to the missionaries, Tasker had been told. They'd often spent years in the forest and desert places, with the shy and wary bands who tucked themselves away from the rest of the world in the hope that they would be forgotten and found to their dismay that there was always somebody who would treat this as a challenge—which didn't always go well for the missionaries. The lucky ones were introduced to the pleasures of mosquitoes, ten-klick scrub marches and long days of digging for tubers; the unlucky ones didn't return. The Karvag Institute might be in the middle of nowhere with none of the entertainments of civilisation and a strenuously blasphemous attitude towards the scientific method but it was at least comfortable, and work with the blackfin no more dangerous, strenuous or uncomfortable than any sea journey. To a missionary, the sheer strangeness of the blackfin was a more enjoyable kind of challenge than trying to guess whether their hosts were joking about the human sacrifices. For Tasker, it posed a set of problems to contend with in explaining to them why he wanted to affix metal contraptions to their heads and send them diving to the bottom of the fjord.

It would have been much easier, too, if he knew more about blackfin biology than he'd been trying to rapidly learn. Tasker was an ichthyologist by trade. Coming from a family of merchants and occasional artisans rather than born to the Academics and inducted as a student in his mid-teens, he might be at a disadvantage against those born and raised to science, but—without family obligations to carry on—Tasker had been free enough to choose his own field of work. Maybe because he'd always loved the ocean, and maybe because he'd always feared it, he'd been drawn to the study of its depths and made a speciality of deep-water fish. It was important to keep track of what was down there, otherwise fishermen would skirt the quotas and the denizens of the deep would end up in the fish-market and exotic pet trade, with potential ramifications across the ocean ecosystem: that was the formal justification for his work. Tasker had always, privately, hoped to find something spectacular—the ocean still held secrets, did it not?—but this was not something for an Academy Member to say out loud.

He'd thought, if he could not make great discoveries like the ancient scientists, he could at least develop a more effective way to perform the surveys—and nose around the infamous Karvag Institute in the process. Currently the Academy was giving the Institute the cold shoulder (which was more pointed here in Karvag than it had been in the south; Tasker had a distinct sense of people not using words like "schism") and had placed sanctions on collaboration until such time as the Institute recanted its mission statements. So Tasker had lobbied in København until the Dean referred him to Lyon, and there lobbied the Senior Dean until she agreed to an interview.

"I assume you have not forgotten the third tenet," she'd said. (In Classic English; but that was how it translated.)

"It is scientifically incorrect to engage in useless speculation."

She'd looked down her nose at him: Tasker in his finest clothes, the best kneel he could manage, painfully aware of his own breathing in the silent office-hall.

"And the eighth and ninth?"

"A sapient species must not be confused for a non-sapient species. The modern human is the only living sapient species."

"So let it be proven."

"So let it be proven," Tasker had echoed, and remained kneeling until one of the minor deans at the side of the hall coughed and made a frantic gesture. Then the Senior Dean had smiled, and granted him permission.

Why muck around with ocean probes when a cetacean could manoeuvre more effectively, would make intelligent decisions, and was less likely to break down at the first sign of squid ink or disturbed mud? Nobody had tried it with much success, but nobody else had been able to speak to the subjects: and that would be a great help in figuring out teething problems.

This was an activity that required a lot more active interaction from the blackfin than many visitors asked for, and in the end only Sundsvall was eager. Wick, with all the logic of a traditionalist, had no objection to letting Mella pin a translator to the side of her son's jaw (as had been done for generations) but was leery of these new and strange toys. Paris was simply uninterested in what she called show-off diving. She claimed it would hurt her ears—and she'd always, Mella said, been the least likely of the blackfin to do something for the sake of curiosity, and the most likely to resent human presumption. After a long and meandering conversation one day, Tasker, paddling back to the dock, thought that he'd be resentful too if an alien species spent generations hunting and harassing humans before some of its members decided they wanted to be friends, where "friendship" meant treating people as research subjects. (Tasker was sharp enough to know a hypothetical when he heard one and had refrained from explaining to Paris that this was never likely to become a reality. The ancient scientists had conclusively proven against the likelihood of finding complex life on other planets. There had been a few fringe Academics over the centuries who insisted on continuing the search, usually out of their own pockets after they were swiftly booted from the Academy for spouting gibberish. There had been a more concerted effort during the reign of Philip the Proud as a compromise against a mission to the Moon; at least telescopes could be used for sunspot monitoring. Tasker suspected the recent strident attitude against the possibility of so-called-aliens was partly out of embarrassment over this blip in the Academy's otherwise proud, non-kowtowing history. People who pointed out that complex life had to exist somewhere in the Universe were greeted with the same sort of exasperated amusement as a child who said there would be no wars if people stopped fighting, or a government official who suggested poor people would be better off if they got jobs and worked hard. It might be true but it wouldn't get the bread baked. The concept of a "planet" was a bit beyond the blackfin, anyway.)

"You're splashing," said Mella. Tasker grunted and tried to keep his paddle strokes in time, but in his current mood it would have been hard enough to keep the paddle under control if he'd had any skill to begin with. Mella glanced over her shoulder and waved at him to stop. "What is it?"

"Paris is right," he said. "She's right. I don't even know why I'm—how I can justify asking this of them. What are they asking from us? All they want is to be left alone and they shouldn't have to ask that, we should never have . . . They're not getting anything back and they don't care about what's at the bottom of the bloody ocean and I—I—what's the point?"

As he came to the end of this, it occurred to Tasker that maybe he'd gone too far. Mella worked with the blackfin. She was Academy-born, and Academic children grew up with the tenets as bedtime stories. A sapient species must not be confused for a non-sapient species. The modern human is the only living sapient species. Mella respected the blackfin, she cared for them—but she did work with them. She took the researchers out to probe and prod at them. She might well be defensive about her role in their exploitation.

He expected her, at the least, to have a lot to say. Mella usually did.

Instead she gave him a wry half-smile and all she said was, "Good."

It would be rude, Tasker thought, to demand an explanation to a cryptic statement. By that Sixday the broader dilemma had almost managed to push Mella's unhelpful comment out of his mind; and if it hadn't, the morning's post certainly did.

The dining hall was quiet when a clerk scurried in with an armful of letters and parcels. He handed a copy of the Bergen Times to a couple of students and another along with a bundle of official-looking envelopes to Mella's father. The most recent journals were stacked neatly at the end of the long table, and two envelopes landed next to Tasker's smoked salmon.

His sister had sent him a letter and, folded into the envelope, a painting on soft linen cloth. Tasker stretched it out to remove the creases and showed to Mella a stylised image of the Roskilde temple, accented with beads and black-thread embroidery. The painting would need to be ironed out and mounted on a frame for any kind of display, but that was preferable to the expense of having it shipped already mounted all the way up here. The accompanying letter told Tasker that she'd done the painting to give herself a break from a particularly dull commission, that her fiancé had unintentionally dyed his hair blue (he'd been aiming for green), and that she hoped the weather was as good in Vestlanorge as it was in Sjælland.

Tasker spent longer poring over the letter than he might have, because he knew the other was going to be tiresome. The envelope was of finer paper than would have been sensible for the bumpy journey, which had left it scuffed and crumpled. This was enough for Tasker to guess it was from København. When he turned the envelope over, the holographic seal of the Academy confirmed it.

"You're going to have to open that, you know," said Mella, holding the painting up to catch light through the fine weave, and Tasker rolled his eyes and did.

It was bad enough that the letter had been written in Classic English, the preferred language for academic communication among a select and declining few. Tasker tended to stick to Nordic in the hope that people would catch on; Mella couldn't read it at all. She spoke Anglic perfectly well and good Scots, but the rude habit letters had of jumping around on the page when Mella tried to read them made literacy enough of a struggle in Nordic, and nobody spoke Classic English these days: Doctor Ebbeson, who shared Tasker's opinion that it was as useful as Latin or Aramaic, had sensibly left it out of Mella's education. Tasker read the letter out for her, fumbling through a translation as he went.

The University was pleased to hear from him—all being well—as arranged—they would be sending a senior colleague to confirm and evaluate his findings. Judging by the dates, the man was about a week away, and he would stay at the Institute for Tasker's final week and leave with him—as previously discussed.

None of this was what made Tasker put his head on the table.

"Ibsen," he said. "They're sending Ibsen."

"You don't like Ibsen?"

"There are things at the bottom of the ocean that don't like Ibsen." Tasker got along with him particularly badly—Ibsen treated the tenets with an adoration that bordered on religious piety, and Tasker did not—but the man's abrasive personality meant even other zealots had been known to duck into dark corners when they spotted him coming.

Mella patted his hand. She withdrew it before the gesture could be interpreted as anything other than professional, and Tasker raised his head again with a grateful smile. He thought about the long days ahead, the embrace of cool water while the sun burned overhead, the blackfin's smooth skin beneath his hands while he fumbled with devices and electronics that stopped working exactly when they were needed, straps that broke, results that were ruined by a squall or couldn't be repeated or simply made no sense, and always Sundsvall's refusal to listen, Wick's worry, her calf's habit of nosing into everything, and Paris's concerns ringing in his mind. . . . And Mella's teasing laugh and reassurance, the water sparkling and, blended with the certainty that he wouldn't rather be anywhere else, the knowledge that soon he would be.

The following day, at least, Tasker had a reprieve. At the Institute, Freeday meant a day off. Tasker hadn't known what to do with himself for the first few weeks, after Mella and Doctor Ebbeson both insisted that a day off was a day off whatever they did down south. This week, he had plans.

He was dressed early and joined Mella at the dock to catch the first ferry to Kristiansund down the coast. Kristiansund, nestled in another fjord, was the nearest decent-sized town to the Institute. In a more densely-populated region it would have been considered barely more than a village but here in the isolated north it was large enough to have its own arena and nurses' surgery, and some of the Institute students traipsed down during the week to teach the older children the foundations of science. The arena, their destination, stood about half a mile's climb from the town centre through green meadows occupied by ruminating cows and fields of mixed crops. The earth structure had been dug into the hillside so that only the front was constructed of thick stone walls, which were currently plastered over with posters for various shows and concerts: a new translation of Pericles, a new-harmonics troupe on tour and a debate about secular schooling (SOLD OUT). Sand martins darted in and out of nests in the embankment. Tasker watched them flutter around people's heads while Mella negotiated for tickets.

This afternoon they weren't here to see one of the travelling exhibits Tasker remembered as a great joy of childhood. The stalls had been cleared away and a display of old and reconstructed instruments set up. Exhibits on history rather than technology or biology were passably common nowadays—this one had placated the local lecturers by including a few lessons on sound waves and neurology. It was a quiet day: there were about as many members of staff as visitors. The re-enactors who had brought the exhibit together were the expected mix of historians, storytellers and travelling museum curators, along with a couple giving demonstrations who seemed to be first and foremost musicians. A small crowd had gathered around the old man playing the hardingfele. He had the slightly awkward air and lax attitude towards style common in folk-academics and he wasn't the only one with that undersocialised, unfashionable look, though several others were quite unremarkable and one girl might not have looked out of place showing off at the Queen's court.

Most of the visitors were townsfolk, with a handful of farmers' families among them. One little boy tugged at his mother's hand and pointed up to a looping leather tube taller than he was set up next to its rotting companion. "Mama, what's that?"

The mother looked around in a fluster. There were no staff members nearby. "I don't know, love." They both used the light Romsdal dialect, and Tasker remembered that—though recognisably related to Nordic when spoken—Romsdal speakers had never adopted the New Alphabet. Some had learned, of course; but this woman, who looked like a farmer, obviously couldn't read the sign.

"It's a serpent," said Tasker, reading it out for her. "First played in France to accompany the choir, in fifteen-ninety—that's almost two thousand years ago," he added. The mother flashed him a grateful smile and translated haltingly for the boy. Tasker wondered if she would attend the education debate. How would she feel about being told her son should learn Nordic, at the expense of Romsdal's own writing and literature?

He listened to the demonstrations for a while, but after a few minutes they started to loop through the same simple pieces and he grew bored. There were limits to Tasker's engagement with motionless artefacts accompanied by dry descriptions, no matter how interesting the history of those instruments. While Mella struck up a conversation with one of the re-enactors, Tasker wandered through the room again and tried to guess when the original instruments dated to without reading the signs, whether they'd been banned by the Munich Reformed Church, and then more creatively how they might be advertised as weapons of war. He had retreated to the piled earth benches of the circle and found a place in the sun to read—the same nursery rhymes still drifting up to catch his ears—when Mella finally came looking for him.

"It's not boring," he said. "I just . . ."

Mella waved away his objections as she sat down. "It's fine. Exhibits aren't everybody's thing." She leaned back with her elbows on the floor of the row behind and stretched her legs out to catch the sun. Tasker, a little distracted by her legs and the sun in Mella's sea-bleached hair, tried to go back to reading. He jumped when Mella spoke again.

"It never occurs to a lot of people that what we do could be seen as exploitative. I mean . . . what you want to do, you're asking a lot of the blackfin, but it's also not the first time Paris has kicked off like that. And, yes, we probably do take more than we give." She tilted her head back, up to the clear blue sky. "Not by being friends with them, not by talking to them. That's different. It's equal."

"The tenets claim they're not equal."

"All that means is the ancients believed they weren't. We can do better now.

Don't you think?"

She said this last with a cheeky grin. Tasker clamped his hands over his ears. "I am a good Academy Member and I will not listen to this nonsense." He lifted his near hand. "Continue."

"It's one thing being friends with them. But by treating them as research objects—yes, sometimes I do wonder how we can justify that."

"Then how do you?"

Mella flashed him a mirthless smile. "I'm a research object myself, you know. The girl who talks to whales. Though they're not—" She seemed to stop herself. She knew she didn't need to explain to him, Tasker thought, the difference between a blackfin and a whale. "People don't know, and they don't understand, and I think . . . if we let the research happen, if we let all the linguists and sociologists and everybody else do their studies and tell people about them then more people understand—how similar they are to us, and that they deserve to be treated well. And I know that brings it round to giving them no choice in the matter again, but . . ."

"But they don't have a choice," said Tasker, trying to muddle it out. "They're not the same as us. We can't make them want to do the research, for the same reasons we want to—and right now I'm not sure those are worth anything—"

Mella laughed.

"They shouldn't have to think the same way we do, but as long as they won't—as long as they can't—and as long as humans are the ones with all the power in the equation, which we always are, then we have to protect them," she said, and Tasker thought of the drowned whaling ship. "Which sometimes means forcing them, and nobody likes being told it's for their own good. Anyway, it's not like they're never interested. You know Sundsvall is. Wick, too, when she's not fussing over her baby. They like to be told about the research reports. They'll want to be told what you find, when you go, and how you're getting on. If you've managed to make the big whales cooperate, or if they've given you the capsizing you deserve, is how Paris put it."

"You're not interested, then?" Tasker said.

Mella flushed. "Obviously. I like reading the reports too. I like thinking that we're reminding people how insignificant and uninteresting they really are. Humans need to be reminded of that. I think that—that helps us too, maybe."

The second tenet came to Tasker's mind: It is scientifically correct to claim the modern human species is special or exceptional.

"It has before."

"Yeah."

Tasker slipped a marker into his book. "What did you mean by 'good'?"

"You figured it out on your own," said Mella, sitting up. "Well, with Paris's help—but Paris is one of the blackfin. You didn't need me or Dad or any of the others to explain it to you. Usually people do, and when Academy Members still came Dad says usually they wouldn't listen even after they were told. I'm almost proud."

Tasker thought of people coming to the Institute and being infected with new ideas—or were they old ones? He thought of the place seeding itself and spreading its tendrils across the continent. Not long ago you'd needed Classic English to get anywhere in the world: now you needed Nordic, and the Karvag Institute had supported itself for decades without the Academy's help, and if they'd infected him with heresy here he didn't think he minded.

"Well, when you think that when I arrived here I was a helpless boy who couldn't hold a paddle . . ."

"And still can't."

Tasker gave her a shove. "Hush, you."

"You've done some good work here, too. Ibsen will be—well, if he doesn't think so, I'll push him in the fjord." It was Tasker's turn to laugh.

They were thrown out for an hour while the exhibition was cleared away, then filed back in to join the growing crowd now forming an audience in front of the curtained stage. It was a warm night. The sun hung low among wispy clouds at the edge of the sky, and the managers had decided not to raise the canvas tent over the arena. Staff members passed programmes along the rows while the musicians fussed around trying to get their instruments in order.

"What do you think they'd make of this?" asked Tasker.

"Interesting from an anthropological perspective, but that human music has no intrinsic artistic value." Mella gave him a sideways look. "I'm paraphrasing."

"Who said that?"

"All of them."

Ibsen's arrival went no worse than might have been expected. Nobody made the foolish suggestion of letting him actually speak with the blackfin. Doctor Ibsen was a senior oceanographer who, when not reciting the tenets, thought in salinity levels, oxygen isotopes and deepwater currents. He treated humans and non-humans alike with a brusque dismissiveness, and spent more of the week trawling through the data than haranguing anybody at the Institute (other than a few terrified clerks). To Tasker's relief, he concluded there were no serious faults to be found in either his method or his preliminary conclusions, which had been scoured of the faintest hint of heresy, and Ibsen seemed almost approving. Or at least, not disapproving. That meant Mella didn't have to push him in the fjord, though at one point she mimed doing so behind his back, and Tasker stifled his laughter too late to keep the man from noticing. He decided not to worry about it. Ibsen already thought he was unprofessional. Ibsen thought everybody was unprofessional. Ibsen sometimes thought equipment was being unprofessional.

The week passed too quickly. Soon Tasker found he had packed his bags and that it was his last day at Karvag. The wind was up, but Mella threw an oilskin at him and they took the kayak as far out into the fjord as they dared, where they found the blackfin without much difficulty. Mella slipped from the boat and ducked under the surface to meet Wick's baby. She gave his mother a shove when Wick nudged in close, and only succeeded in pushing herself away from the adult's great bulk.

"Go on," she said to Tasker, when she'd climbed back into the kayak.

Tasker handed her an earpiece and played around with the controls until he'd managed to tune in to a brand-new channel. The excited, almost unintelligible voice of Wick's baby filled both their ears.

"Mamma! Mamma! Me being-is being-is here-here-here-here!"

Mella laughed, then set about trying to get the baby to slow down. "All aright be, Hillerød."

"Hillerød?"

"Don't get a big head. You're not the first."

When the blackfin had gone, Tasker pulled the earpiece off with a pang of grief. He tried to twist to look back as they paddled for shore and sent his blade skimming wildly over the water instead of neatly through.

Mella huffed. "If you can't concentrate, don't bother."

But they were gone. The tall dark fins had vanished into the choppy waves. Tasker put his head down and focused on paddling half-decently. At the boathouse, once they'd pulled the kayak up, they both hovered for a moment as if there was something else to say—then exchanged tight smiles and hurried up the path, under strengthening rain, to the Institute's main buildings. That evening they found themselves the last people in the dinner hall, lingering, unwilling to leave, until Mella said, "Do you like Anglic wine?"

"I don't think I've ever tried it."

"Well, we've got to fix that. Come on." Mella led him by the hand to her room where, over most of a bottle of remarkably good rosé, she told Tasker about her father's most recent project: taking on the Nordic government. "He's lobbying to have the blackfin—all whales and dolphins, if possible—recognised as persons under NU law."

That would make whaling an act of multiple homicide, and a capital offence. "I like the sound of that."

"It means raising an assembly."

Yes, it did. The mainstream of the Academy would not like that at all. "The

Karvag Institute? Against the Deans?"

"We've got a few universities on side, and probably the NU if they're brave enough to take on the Academy." She smiled. "But we could always use friends."

Tasker thought: schism. Mella had never been to Gothenburg or Lyon. She wasn't fool enough to believe the tenets could be amended—that hadn't happened in almost a thousand years; it was the stuff of history—but she might believe they would be quietly ignored. It was a thing that happened in the north. Karvag might have gone furthest in heresy, with other small Institutes following in its wake, but a couple of the universities were playing their own balancing game of by turns provoking and flattering the legislative heart of the Academy. Tasker's København was more flexible than he'd seen or guessed at in Lyon. If this were to continue—

Another breakaway from the core Academy? An Academy which abandoned the eighth and ninth tenets, and offered the blackfin the status they deserved? Was it possible?

"I'm in," said Tasker.

He topped up both their wine cups, then frowned at the small amount remaining in the bottle. Mella nodded as if she wouldn't have expected anything less. "So you'll have to keep up to date with what's going on here. You'll have to write, won't you?" She wore a triumphant expression, like she'd backed him into some kind of corner. Tasker was tempted to laugh. He settled for kissing her.

He'd spilled the wine, but that didn't matter, because her skin smelled of salt and her eyes were the blue-grey of a northern sea and he was leaving tomorrow and, most importantly, she'd kissed him back.

The following morning (only barely hungover) he and Ibsen said stiff farewells to the people of the Institute, with a hearty handshake from Doctor "Call me Karl" Ebbeson and a brief, formal one from Mella herself. Tasker liked to think the goodbyes were stiff for Ibsen because they were relieved to see the back of him, and for himself because they would miss him—but perhaps he was kidding himself. Perhaps all the people of the Institute were eager for this ignorant southern boy to leave so they could get back to their proper jobs. Except for Mella, of course, who teased him that Sundsvall would mourn his departure more than she did and made him promise again to write. They said no more than this. Displays of affection in public, except between parent and child, were considered improper even among layfolk—more so here in the north than in the south, or maybe here in the countryside than in the cities—and would be highly inappropriate for two Academy Members. Tasker had to settle for a quiet nod.

Then, in the manner of all big things, it was somehow small. Tasker took a few steps onto the Bergen ferry and watched the rope cast off, and the Institute vanished behind the hills. The days blurred into weeks, into months, into a sodden winter of long days indoors in København working out the kinks in the methods Tasker had developed and the ways they would need to be modified for the studies everybody in the oceanography department thought of as the real subject of interest. A long winter: the others in the oceanography department were friendlier than Ibsen but no less strait-laced, and there were none of them Tasker could easily talk to. They worked in a field which had answered all its questions, he thought— why would they mind the constraints of the tenets? How far did they realise the methods they were so excited about had become possible because somebody else had flouted them?

Tasker tried to be excited too. Maybe they would learn something. The ocean floor was well-mapped but he believed it still held mysteries, and it was hardly heresy if you stumbled across them by accident. He must keep quiet about the new kinds of thoughts swirling round in his head; he had pushed his luck with the University at Lyon already.

So he did not run back to Karvag like a character in a bad romantic serial. Instead, the following March, he caught a much larger boat across the wide ocean, then another down the drowned Florida coast to the warm Caribbean. There the sun was always bright but the day-lengths barely changed, and Tasker was obliged to speak in rusty Ispanian, and the tropical waters danced blue-green and drunken monkeys stole rum from his glass if he didn't pay attention. There Tasker learned his way around a refitted fishing boat and a coastal town with thriving nightlife, which he enjoyed enough that he was often nursing a headache when they took the boat out in the morning. Ibsen, who could not be shaken off even by crossing the Atlantic, would glower and chide him, but the others laughed and Tasker laughed with them. They needed laughter, because for a week they criss-crossed the empty sea with no sign of their quarry. These creatures were not Mella's blackfin. They did not come when called.

Then one afternoon the captain whistled a stop and dropped anchor, and everybody on the boat held their breath while they waited to see if it had been another false alarm. Tasker gripped the wooden railing hard enough to give himself splinters. Sunlight glanced off the water.

The true giants of the ocean dwarfed Mella's blackfin. They were the largest creatures on Earth, they dove unequalled distances, they had the biggest brains of any species ever known—

All of these facts were pushed from Tasker's head in sheer awe as the sperm whale emerged from the depths.

‡‡

The next time Tasker saw Mella was not in Karvag but in Uppsala, two years later, at a conference of the Queen's court. Experts had travelled from across Europe to throw their weight in on a discussion of Doctor Ebbeson's proposals. Tasker still struggled to believe he was counted among them. He was only a junior fellow in København, but he was also (it turned out) the world's foremost sperm whale trainer—largely by dint of being the first one. Sometimes even he forgot his work was really in deepwater fish.

Tasker's turn to speak came on the third morning. "Don't worry about it," Mella said, in a brief meeting before the day started. "You'll be fine." Naturally, Tasker instead dropped his notes in front of several important Deans and a couple of minor royals, stammered out a statement and sank back down onto the plush bench wishing he could sink right through it. There was a prince! As a merchant's son from the staunchly timocratic League cities, Tasker had never imagined he would address a prince: it was much less of an honour than meeting the Senior Dean, but somehow far stranger. And he'd utterly embarrassed himself.

Mella flashed him a smile from the court benches.

At noon they were dismissed to allow the Council to deliberate. Mella grabbed Tasker by the arm and steered him away before he could be caught up in the conversation.

"I don't want to talk about it," she said, marching him sharply towards the market.

"Mussels?" said Tasker.

They bought lunch at a stall (fresh mussels, piping hot) and settled on the stone edge of a fountain to eat. "Do you think they'll—"

"What did I say?" She paused, seeming to realise she'd spoken too sharply. "Sorry."

"Me too."

"It's not just—I'm worried about Sundsvall too. I know I can't help, but I don't like being away from her . . ."

"How's she getting on?" asked Tasker, recalling from the letters (which were nothing compared to sight and sound, and this the first chance he'd had to really talk to Mella in the whirl of organisation over the last half-week) that Sundsvall was heavily pregnant. The conversation moved from there to a general discussion of both blackfin and human life, as it went on, up at the Institute. Mella was still jittery, one leg thrumming up and down, and though the mussels were delicious she'd barely managed to force down half the bowl. Tasker, who'd spent the morning in acute awareness of his imminent botch-up and struggled to eat breakfast, finished them for her. In his turn he told Mella what more he'd learned about the success of their work—they could learn more in a day with a camera-armed sperm whale than in a month with a probe—and the creatures of the deep ocean. Beautiful they might be, but they were harder to love than the massive, vulnerable whales and blackfin. It seemed an intrusion even to look into their world.

A child tossed a silver coin into the fountain. The splash sent ripples shimmering outwards. They bounced off the stone edge, into themselves, and faded to nothing. Their reflections were washed of colour in the mirror-still water, close next to each other and darkened by the spring sun.

"What will you do if the proposal passes?" asked Tasker. "Are you ready to take on the Academy in assembly?" The Senior Dean had made it clear she would not stand for letting the NU pass heretic laws—not while it remained under the aegis of the Academy. Three things might happen: the NU split from the Academy, as the Anglians had once done; or the Academy split from within; or its central power structures be overthrown. None of those would be pretty. Tasker thought they'd won the rational argument, but the court might well strike down the proposal simply to avoid the consequences.

The child went running back to her mother. Mella gave Tasker her patented you're-an-idiot look. "That was always the point."

"It was, wasn't it?" he said. "You know, I can think of a few people outside the NU who might be convinced you're the better bet. People who'd be interested in talking to you."

Mella tilted her head. "Since you went rogue, I think Lyon's less interested than ever in letting us Institute folks near the faithful."

That was putting it mildly. The only things saving the Karvag Institute from outright expulsion were the number of Universities that would need to be expelled with it, and the Senior Dean's unwillingness to admit she had lost control of the situation.

"Oh, there are ways around that. You could write a book, maybe."

"A book? You want me to write a book?" Mella looked half-curious, half-sceptical. Tasker thought it probably hadn't occurred to her, the girl who hated reading and had never learned anything from ink and paper.

"Maybe you could do with a partner. Someone who can handle academic writing." He paused, then added: "And translate Classic English for you. Or you could travel. You might not be able to hold exhibits or seminars, but there are still people who'd want to meet you, in København and Hillerød."

Mella pushed him. She was smiling. "If it passes."

"You know, I think we've really got a very good—"

"Do you want to end up in the fountain?"

"—chance. I'm sure the Queen will—"

She pushed him again, harder, and Tasker went sprawling backwards. In the moment of confusion he reached out and grabbed Mella's jacket, unbalancing her enough to pull her with him so that they both landed with a splash in the cold, stale-tasting water. A cry of, "Mamma! Mamma!" rang out, and Tasker surfaced to see the little girl hopping up and down with glee. "Mamma, they fell in the fountain!"

A couple of market shoppers helped to fish them out. Dripping wet and grinning was a highly undignified position for a fellow of the University of København, so Tasker decided he might as well compound it by planting an inappropriate kiss on Mella's cheek. It was the city, after all. The year's first martins darted round the painted stalls. Somebody tutted at his boldness. Mella only laughed, and Tasker leaned in to speak quietly into her ear.

"The Queen will make the right decision."

"Hush, you."

He wondered if the blackfin too were waiting in impatience for the results of the conference; they'd have longer to wait, whatever happened. He would go back, Tasker had already decided, if not with Mella then when he could, to meet Sundsvall's calf and see how Hillerød had grown, and when he was there he might ask them. Had they understood why Mella had left them, and what she was trying to do? Had they waited, or had they swum unconcerned in their green water, wise as they were, focused only on the swell and running tide while small human boats criss-crossed the water and were gone?

A Change in the Wind

by Jeanne Labonte

To Abbott Aiden Donoghue, New Waterford Abbey, Eire
From Cardinal Dominic Benenati, Turin, Piedmont

The Thirtieth of March, Year of Our Blessed Lord 3015

MAY THE PEACE OF CHRIST be with you, my old friend,

I pray this letter reaches you safely and finds you in good health. News of the terrible winter storm devastating the isles of western Eire was received by radio several months ago. However, I had difficulty determining how grave the situation was. Such information is often distorted or greatly exaggerated by eager transmitters wishing to awe the unlettered with how they snatch information from the very ether long before it arrives by word of mouth or letter. As usual, I had to depend on the accounts of travelers who had actually witnessed the storm. Since your abbey is on the east coast, I hope you were spared the worst of it. One of our archivists recently remarked that there seemed to be fewer of these types of storms than in years gone by, but they certainly have lost none of their ferocity when they do arrive.

Your letter of the 15th of December arrived a few days ago. It does not surprise me to hear that Abbot Padrick Monaghana has finally passed into the comforting arms of our Dear Lord at the marvelous age of ninety-three. His wry wit and clear vision will be greatly missed. I suppose his replacement at the Abbey of Duibhlinn has already been voted in but I fear any successors will suffer in comparison to the Old Abbot for many years to come.

You are right to chide me for not responding to your letter from last summer but as you know, I have been immersed in completing the move of the last of the Vatican Archives from Grenoble to Turin. The hurried flight from Avignon two years ago resulted in the loss of a number of books including a dozen or so old history texts, mostly dating from the twenty-first and twenty-second centuries. While thankfully copies had been made long ago and stored elsewhere, it was still a great sorrow to lose some of the few original machine printed books we have surviving from the Terrible Ages. My suspicion is that they were stolen, and given their fragile condition, I have little hope they will ever be recovered. I was instructed by the Curia to inventory what we had (a considerable task to say the least!) to determine if any other books had been taken and devise a plan to ensure against further chance of theft when it came time to move again.

Unfortunately the poisonous leaks from the old uncharted waste mounds inadvertently breached by the Mornantia Commune still continue. Our cartographers have updated their maps to mark the site, but too late for those who live downriver. Currently several of the Rhone tributary waters still have the stink of contamination and will not be fit for drinking or fishing for some time to come. In fact, according to my Essene contact in the Vaucluse Kingdom, not only does Avignon remain nearly abandoned out of terror of the dreadful chemical toxins but even many of the unaffected surrounding villages are deserted. The searing memories of the radiant poisons of Blayais and their horrible effects still linger even after many generations so the slightest hint of any sort of pollution sends people fleeing. So the final decision was made to move all to Turin as there are buildings already suitable for storing archives in the ancient city.

Naturally, there has been talk (once again!) of reestablishing the Holy Vatican See at its original seat in Rome now that the petty salvage-lords plaguing the southern peninsula have at long last been stamped out. But as anyone venturing into the battered remnants of that city realizes quickly, rebuilding the Church to anything approaching its former extravagant glory would be a hopeless effort in these resource-poor times and certainly not a wise use of the minds and hands God gave us. But still, the grass-covered remains of what was once Saint Peter's Basilica would break the heart of any Christian who has seen the few old surviving drawings showing it in its prime. The chaos of the Terrible Ages, earthquakes, salvage raiders from the east and south combined with sea storms over many centuries all have worked to reduce that one-time magnificent building to something its creators would no longer recognize. All is impermanent, as the Buda folk say.

Since you have a radio receiver at your abbey, you undoubtedly know that once again we have been treated to a diatribe broadcasted by the drooling senile imbeciles—oh, pardon!—the venerable, glorious Fifth Reich of Deutschland! Are you not in awe, my old friend? The saviors of civilization (as they would have us believe) have seen fit to warn us YET again of the dangers of recommencing trade with the nefarious Americans from across the ocean. Never mind the extreme difficulties of travel across the Atlantic. Never mind that the United States has not existed as a nation for nearly nine hundred years and is only remembered by scholars. Never mind that the trade in question has only been with the common-wealths of New Boston and New York. Or that the Janeiro River City-State is not even located on the northern continent. (Do these people not look at their atlases?) No, my dear Aiden, it is clear to any person of intelligence that the Americans are determined to reestablish their former hegemony over us all by luring us into bartering for such tempting but worthless trifles as amaranth grain, tobacco, cider, bolts of cotton, hemp paper and rope, bicycles—with rubber tires, no less! (Oh, the perfidy of it all. . . .) Something tells me that the Reich will never get over the loss of its monopoly on book printing.

Perhaps it is fortunate that the old Cortes of Espania has died childless and the withered remnants of his country are being methodically carved up by the king-doms of Portugali and Valenci as well as the Catalonian Principality. (It will be in-teresting to see how long that process remains amiable!) Otherwise I am sure he also would fire off a cannonade of his own absurdly antiquated rhetoric in an effort to outshout the Reich or worse, have his long-suffering peasants parade at his borders in imitation of the war maneuvers that the ancients used to engage in when they felt the need for saber rattling. In all honesty, I am not certain that the increasing spread of the use of radio is the unalloyed blessing its preservers would have us be-lieve. Not when we have to listen to nonsense like this.

Still, I suppose we may be grateful for the continued existence of the glorious Reich. That they have lasted as long as they have can be taken as a sign that the Ukrani, Kazakhs, Belrooz and other eastern barbarians have become far too en-feebled eternally battling with each other as well as their southern neighbors to be a threat to us any longer or they surely would have overrun that sclerotic remnant of an earlier age by now, doubtless with the aid of push brooms.

Forgive me; I am getting too facetious in my old age, am I not? You know well how much I love to rant about the Reich. No doubt you would much prefer to hear about the visitors we recently had. I was very fortunate to be part of the group that met with them and can provide you with a firsthand account. It was by chance I was visiting an acquaintance, one Ricardio Gassamai, a book trader who lives in Upper Genoa. You would not know him, Aiden, as he is mildly crippled from polio and prefers to have other book traders come to him rather than attempt traveling in search of them. He had acquired some old handwritten chemistry books and was hopeful of contributing them to the Archives. He believed they might be as early as the twenty-third century as printing presses had nearly disappeared by then, for-cing those copying old books to do so manually. Having done that in my youth, I can recall how tedious a process it was and can only pity the poor scholar trying to rescue the surviving wood pulp books of earlier centuries while they gradually dis-integrated as he or she tried to copy them!

Sadly, I had to disappoint him as the books, while in excellent condition, were forgeries likely dating from the twenty-eighth century. A close examination revealed the artificial aging done to make them appear of great antiquity. The vocabulary, ostensibly written in Old French, had too many anachronistic wordings to be of truly ancient vintage. Also, despite their titles, they were alchemical texts. Since the standards for the Vatican Archives are very strict, particularly when it involves older superstitions instead of the greater Sciences, I was forced to refuse them. It was a pity, as someone had done an excellent job of reproducing the illustrations that often accompanied such texts and the script was very readable. The increasing demand for any works of science in those days encouraged such forgeries, some quite clever. The unknown copyist certainly made it look quite convincing to someone ignorant of the difference between chemistry and alchemy. Sadly, there was and still is confusion between the greater Sciences and the false sciences. It takes an experienced scholar to distinguish the precious stones from the mere rubbish and I am embarrassed to admit even I have been deceived on occasion.

While we were mulling over what to do with the books, a young apprentice wearing the brown sash of the Genoan Fire Suppression Guild arrived in search of me. He was tremendously excited, for the most part over having been entrusted to bring a message. Prattling at a great rate, he went on about mysterious invaders by the islands and strange boats speaking Old English before I could get him to calm enough to explain that a radio message from a returning sea captain about having captured some ships of unknown origin near some islands (sadly, the lad had already forgotten the name) had been received by the Genoan ruling council. Suspecting I was getting some sort of garbled story regarding the efforts of the Piedmont and Toscana navies in assisting the Venezians combating the piracy plaguing the Adriatic, and more than a little puzzled as to why I was being summoned, I had the lad escort me to the Palazzo.

Arriving there, my confusion began clearing when I was told that far from being captured, the unknown boats in question had actually been rescued. Evidently while scouting near the Corfu islands, a Captain Ricci, of the Genoan ship Martello, encountered two Govina pirate vessels attempting to board a trio of curious ships, the design unfamiliar to him. Quickly ordering his sailors to fire off the two cannons they were equipped with, they were able to frighten away the smaller pirate ships. The raiders had set fire to one of the unknown vessels so the captain at once ordered a rescue.

The men and women plucked from the burning ship appeared to Captain Ricci, to be possibly Southern Mediterranean, as their vessels' sails were decorated with what he recognized was Arabic lettering and their garb similar to that worn by the Szunizian and Tuarheg people eking out a living along the coasts of Old Tunis and Algeria. He was astonished, as none of the people of that region had any sea-going capability he was aware of other than small fishing craft. However, they did not seem to understand when he spoke to them. Their language was quite unfamiliar when they tried to communicate with him in turn. One fellow did seem to speak more than one language, one of which sounded like Old English, though knowing only a few words of that tongue, the captain could not be sure. Since they seemed willing to accompany him, he then set sail back to Genoa guiding the two remaining ships. I became intrigued and suspected the strangers had actually come from some part of the Libyan coast. The Genoan governor, a well-educated man, wondered as much himself so he sent out a summons to any priests or scholars possessing knowledge of Old English hoping to communicate with them.

Another who had answered the summons was Bishop Matteo DiPietro, who I met once when he was researching the historical section of the Vatican Archives. He is a small stout man who moves and gestures with great energy. His deep interest was in tracing the migration routes of the varied peoples inhabiting the lands to the east and south, a daunting task to my thinking as archive records are fragmentary and contradictory given the chaos both political and environmental tormenting those lands during the Terrible Ages. Discussion immediately began as to who the strangers might be.

He quickly disputed my theory they might be Libyans, convinced the ancient wars, epidemics and vicious heat waves of the Terrible Ages had depopulated that land beyond hope of recovery. It was his opinion, given the location they were encountered, that they actually were from the northeastern Mediterranean: Circassia, Turkey, or even possibly some remnant of the Aleppan Caliphate (if it still existed after so many centuries). Given the persistent Govina and Zarba raiders from the east Adriatic shores who make any trade with the Grecian peninsula irregular at best, the little information we had about any lands beyond was largely suspect. He pointed out the occasional contacts with the Szuniz coastal people certainly never brought any hint of trade with Libyans capable of building boats, the lack of wood being Matteo's most convincing argument. We reluctantly agreed that we would have to wait and see what the Martello brought us. As the ship was not expected to arrive for a few more days, the governor was kind enough to provide lodgings for Matteo, who had only been visiting the city for the day. Ricardio was more than willing to have me stay a while longer, expressing the hope he might accompany me to greet the strangers.

On the day the boats arrived, we went down to the harbor, on being informed of the Martello's docking after we had returned from morning services. The weather seemed auspicious, with bright sunshine and a brisk warm breeze. Word of mouth had attracted numerous onlookers, crowding near the docks in an effort to glimpse the strangers. The Genoan council had brought in several Piedmont soldiers with the idea of having them urge people to move along, concerned the newcomers might be alarmed or feel overwhelmed. I was surprised the council went to the trouble as the crowd was well behaved, intense curiosity being the main emotion. So the soldiers had little to do, occupying themselves instead with eating food provided by an enterprising vendor or staring at the Martello and the accompanying strangers, one fellow actually peering through a spyglass while seated on some fishing nets. The governor, spotting Ricardio and myself, waved us past the soldiers.

Bishop DiPietro had already arrived and hurried up to us nearly beside himself with delight, declaring the boats could only be of Egyptian origin. Both Ricardio and I were dubious at first, since it seemed likely Egypt fared no better than Libya in the Terrible Ages. The Franciscan Histories recorded that the Nile had failed to reach the Delta by the beginning of the twenty-second century, even with rising sea levels, leaving famine and plagues to finish what war had not. Since no further news of its people's fate was recorded by Vatican or Deutshlandic archivists, the collapse of that ancient river valley civilization must surely have been complete.

Yet, when we saw the boats, similar to caravels, resting quietly beside the Martello, their sails were boldly decorated with images of the pyramids, Arabic script encircling them—an unmistakable sign of their origin. Where had the wood come from? Had trading somehow managed to resume? With whom? The boats themselves were far smaller than the Martello. Little wonder the Govina pirates thought them easy prey! How had they managed to come so far? Matteo didn't think they could have crossed open water but would have had to hug the coast. Had they really dared to pass the ghastly radiant holes that once had been Tel Aviv and the Holy City? My dear Aiden, I'm sure you can imagine our impatience to meet these people and find out beyond all doubt who they were!

While waiting, we spoke among ourselves, Ricardio pointing out that the depiction of pyramids were images, something historical records indicated was forbidden among the Middle Eastern Islamic cultures. The Szuniz and Tuarheg had no images but used geometric shapes in their art. Matteo suggested that the old records might not be fully accurate as they all too often generalized to the point of error. After a millennium, who could say what the truth was? We could see the governor, who had boarded the Martello, speaking to a small group of people, gesturing extravagantly, his trailing sleeves flapping in the breeze, clearly inviting them ashore. After a moment, he led them down the gangplank while I, my companions, and the crowd behind us all gazed eagerly.

The Egyptians' garments displayed various patterns, with surprisingly bright colors, red being the most common. One fellow, a tall slim man, his dusky face haggard and sallow, broke away from the group and immediately fell to his hands and knees, kissing the ground with obvious joy, much to the astonishment of the spectators. For myself, I easily sympathized with him, being all too familiar with that old ailment, mal-de-mer. A reproving voice came from someone in the midst of the newcomers, and he quickly pulled himself together, dusting off his white and red robe as he rose back to his feet.

Ah, Aiden, how I wish that avid collector (Moishe? Was that his name?) who delighted in acquiring ancient images of the advertising symbols so popular in the era prior to the Terrible Ages, was here. I have no doubt he would have quickly bartered the robe off this man's back, for it was liberally decorated with a recognizable brand name of a popular ancient sweet drink. The dyer of the garment likely saw the bright red curling letters on some relic and thought they would make a fine pattern for the cloth.

Noticing our approach, he eyed us hopefully and began speaking in heavily accented Old English, introducing himself as Youssef Shamoon, interpreter for the Imam of Xandria. Dear me, Aiden. I'm afraid we confused the poor man at first for such was our excitement all three of us began talking at once to him! Fortunately we composed ourselves and appointed Matteo on the spot to do the talking. They conversed very slowly back and forth, for many of the words Youssef used, had changed pronunciation and a few we did not know at all. But that was really no surprise, given their likely isolation and the passage of time. Thankfully, the gist of what he said was comprehensible enough.

Not forgetting our hospitality, we offered Youssef and his group a chance for refreshment and rest after their long arduous voyage, which at first he eagerly accepted, but then caught himself, indicating he would need to consult the Imam first. While he returned to his people, I relayed to the governor our conversation. He, in turn, replied that arrangements had already been made in anticipation of this, adding he had included special instructions for no alcohol, recalling the Islamic ban against it. Pleased at this detail, I turned back to see Youssef returning, accompanied by what could only be the Imam.

The passage of time can perform marvelous alchemies on culture and custom, but none as marvelous as this. For far from being the dour, fearsome, bearded figure that ancient records often spoke anxiously of, instead we found ourselves facing a tiny plump dark skinned woman, perhaps in her seventies, dressed in a bright robe, dyed reddish purple, glittering with glass beads, clutching a walking staff taller than herself. A snow white veil covered her head but left her stern wrinkled face uncovered. Fierce black eyes inspected us with interest. Her interpreter introduced her as Imam Zara.

Through Youssef, she told us our generous offer would be accepted, but asked if we had any physician who might attend one of her scribes, who had suffered a wound on her arm during the pirate attack. I motioned to a nearby guild apprentice (not the same one from a few days before!) and requested that a physician from the local Essene hospital be brought. While I was sure the Martello's doctor was competent enough, my feeling has always been that the Essenes are second to none in their medical ability.

While we awaited the physician, the governor and several dignitaries from the Genoan council led the Egyptians to a shaded arcade, adjacent to the Palazzo, where tables had been set up, with fresh fruit, baked bread and unfermented grape juice. In addition to the Imam and her translator, there were three scribes, two men and a woman, who attended her. The injured scribe, her arm in a sling, looked even paler than Youssef, who she resembled so closely I felt sure they were siblings. There was also a pair of burly guards, armed with spears that looked too ceremonial to be used in combat, the long curved knives tucked in their belts more likely suitable for that. Between them, they carried a small plain wooden chest with a metal latch. The sailors and captain who had piloted their vessels preferred to remain on board to conduct much needed repairs. The mayor sent food and drink out to them, to their obvious appreciation.

The Essene doctor, one Piet Braam, arrived led by the apprentice. Dressed in traditional white, his greying beard neatly trimmed, he was accompanied by a young lad, likely a student, who carried several satchels. As luck would have it, the doctor was fluent in Old English as well, which saved a good deal of translating time. He immediately went to over to tend the young scribe.

In the meantime, we questioned Imam Zara, among other things, asking how she and the others had come to make their hazardous voyage. She began by explaining her people's history. The Nile River had come near to drying up in ages past, according to the Imam, continuing to make its course to the Mediterranean, though sadly much diminished and polluted. She referred to those times as the Age of Suffering, for the population of her land, once great beyond imagining, died off in vast numbers, killed by invaders—or worse, by each other as they struggled over the few resources remaining.

Vivid stories filled her childhood of how armies from the north, the Russhai and the Chinoi battled each other over access to the last of the petroleum in the surrounding lands. So terrible was the fighting, declared the Imam, that Allah Himself finally unleashed His wrath against the Russhai, blasting their army with divine fire as punishment for corrupting the Holy City Jerusalem. He sent the bleeding plague among the Chinoi, in retaliation for their brutal destruction of Holy Mecca, driving all back to their homelands never to return. Her own people were left with nothing but rubble and degrading poverty. The Imam's face grew very sad as she related how learning nearly vanished from her land under the terrible effort just simply to survive. It was plain that Allah had just simply turned His face from them all, due to the unbridled greed for oil and power.

But then, in her eyes, a miracle began occurring, when she was but a very young girl. The Nile, formerly but a sick trickle barely capable of sustaining the people who remained, suddenly began flooding again as it was said to have done in former ages. When it was clear this was a permanent change, the holy imams considered this to be a sign Allah's favor was returning to them. To help heal and restore the land to its former glory, they decided the best way to accomplish this was to revive the old idea of a caliphate. All that remained was to select a suitable leader.

Their choices quickly narrowed to a charismatic sheikh, Mostafa Daher. Governing a group of villages near the ruins of Helwan, he was noted for his efforts in restoring old irrigation channels, reforesting the river banks and building a small school for the local imams. He was greatly respected by all, with many of the other sheikhs along the Great River already deferring to his leadership. By the process of *shura*, both imams and community leaders agreed to have him be the new caliph.

An intelligent, dynamic man, he quickly seized the opportunity offered to him. One of his first acts was to found a new city, located near the newly expanding Delta, calling it Xandria after an ancient famed city of their land. Wisely, rather than waste limited resources coercing surrounding villages into submitting, he built a trade network instead to encourage people to share and expand traditional crafts. The Imam glowingly described how gradually commerce began reviving along the river, crops increased and people began moving to Xandria, attracted by the promise of even a modest prosperity.

Still, there were problems, not the least of which was the lack of wood, which held back their boat building. Only a few species of trees had survived the centuries along the shores of the Nile, not enough to support any extensive construction, and most of the preserved wood of earlier times had been salvaged by previous generations to cook and keep warm. Papyrus was used to make reed boats, but their size and range were very limited. Undaunted, the new Caliph sent out traders into the surrounding lands to the east and south, to establish contacts with their surviving neighbors. Before long, they were able to not only acquire supplies of precious wood but even obtain camels, an animal long absent from their land. Their new alliances proved invaluable when raiders from the southwest (whom the Imam contemptuously referred to as "Wasters") began targeting the newly prosperous Egyptians and needed to be fought off.

The grandson, Mohammad Daher, had recently assumed the title of Caliph. As energetic as his grandfather, and encouraged by the imams, he embarked on the ambitious plan of rebuilding the knowledge their legends said Egypt was famed for. Since many of the nomadic people they traded with were illiterate, this meant they would have to seek beyond the boundaries of the lands they were familiar with.

Now the significance of the Imam's voyage was clear to us. Like the ancient European explorers who sailed in search of spices and gold, the Egyptians sought something they thought far more valuable: regaining a portion of the sciences which allowed our ancestors to accomplish miracles of healing, building, communicating and delving into the secrets of the matchless universe God created. I couldn't help but think of the stingy Reichers, who hoard their countless books like so many medieval dragons, doling out tidbits of knowledge when it suits them to do so.

I asked Imam Zara how they had managed to sail past the radiant areas where, as she put it, God's fire had fallen. She merely smiled and said the fire remnants only threatened those who walked upon the ground. As long as they did not take on fresh water from those shores or eat the fish in the immediate area, sailing past caused no risk. She did admit the captain of her vessel made everyone sit under covers while he piloted his ships as quickly as he could past the dreaded site, a precaution she felt was unnecessary as she was convinced Allah's protection would ensure their safety. I pointed out to her the old adage that it is well to trust Allah but keep your camel tied anyway. This produced a delighted peal of laughter from the old lady.

Their vessels traveled beyond to what sounded to me like the old Syrian coast, where the Aleppan Caliphate once ruled, finding diverse peoples each living in their own small town or village, using both Old English and Old French as common languages. When many, though not openly hostile, refused to allow them to land, they boldly traveled further to discover more friendly people beyond. These told her there was still a great fear of the bleeding plague in many areas, even though there had been no epidemics for nearly a generation. While many they encountered were illiterate, a few small notable places, particularly among the Grecian Isles, still had a vestige of learning so she was able to initiate the beginnings of trade with them. Although at that point the captain wanted to return home, it was at her insistence that they continued westward in spite of the warnings of locals and so ran afoul of the pirates. While she regretted this decision, nevertheless she felt Allah's hand was over them when the Martello rescued them.

Now it was the Imam's turn to ask questions, knowing their information about western lands was greatly outdated. She was disappointed to hear that all of the mighty governments legends spoke of were long dust, in their place countless duchies, kingdoms, communes, districts, confederations, principalities, dominiums and city states of every description. When asked if the Pope still ruled, I explained the Papal throne had been empty for nearly six hundred years, the Church now guided by the Vatican Curia in Turin on which I held the position of Senior Archivist. One question had us momentarily puzzled. She wondered if the Merrakesshans still had a major role in the affairs of Europe. We thought at first she spoke of the former great city in Morocco but it was Matteo who realized she meant the Americans. The confusion was understandable when we saw the crude map one of her scribes brought from their ship. It only showed the Mediterranean and its surrounding lands. The Atlantic was depicted as a narrow tributary of the Mediterranean! When we borrowed the maps the council had at the Palazzo and showed her the true size of the world, she was visibly amazed. Imagine, Aiden, they had forgotten about the existence of Asia and the discovery of the New World! If it hadn't been for our own ancestors diligent efforts to preserve knowledge, we might well have been as ignorant.

By now, the physician was satisfied with the scribe's treatment and recommended she rest for a few days at the Essene hospital to fully recuperate. The Imam and her people, eager to explore the city, readily agreed to this and the governor accepted my offer for me and my companions to guide them. Matteo confided to me that he appreciated giving his hand a rest as he had been avidly recording the Imam's words in the notebooks he had brought with him, having to refill his ink-pot several times. He also voiced a suspicion that the dignified old lady was actually quite conversant in Old English and only employed the interpreter to give herself time to compose her answers to us. As I thought back on our conversations, I too began to suspect this was in fact the case.

The Essene hospital, built of salvaged marble and decorated with stucco, was only a short distance away, nestled amidst herb gardens. It impressed everyone with its peaceful atmosphere and meticulously clean hallways. Doctor Braam explained the disciplines of his order and their long-time dedication not only to the preservation of old medical skills but their efforts to build upon them for the betterment of all people everywhere. Knowing the Egyptians' ambitious search, he indicated their medical schools were open to all individuals, not just simply members of the order and any from her land who might wish to attend could do so without needing to be an Essene. This greatly pleased the Imam.

Youssef, who was indeed the brother of the injured scribe, gazed in delight at the herb gardens after reassuring himself of his sister's wellbeing. He wondered if it were possible to bring back some of the plants to his homeland as everyone in his family dearly loved herbs of every kind. Doctor Braam promised him that plants which could tolerate the hot environment of Egypt would be set aside for him when it came time for him and his sister to return home.

As we stepped back outside, the road outside the hospital bustled with people on their way to vendor markets, along with carts, wagons and small carriages. I heard a startled exclamation from the Imam, and following her gaze, saw a young woman, one of the aristarchs by her dress, nimbly piloting a bicycle between the ox-pulled wagons. It was one of the New Bostonian-made cycles, still a rare luxury down here. With its pedals and rubber tires, the cyclist evidently was unable to resist showing off her new acquisition. To the dismay of her guards, the Imam hurried forward with the clear intention of intercepting the rider.

Fortunately, the young lady, seeing the surprising apparition of Imam Zara approaching her, stopped her bicycle to stare in wonder. When she realized the old lady was curious, she was gracious enough to dismount and begin explaining the workings of the cycle, while I translated to Youssef who in turn translated to the Imam. The guards became increasingly agitated, for it looked at first as if the Imam might want to try out this unusual vehicle. Thankfully, common sense prevailed, as she finally decided at her age such an attempt might not have an auspicious outcome. She marveled at the rubber tires, asking what they were made of, and I explained their origin from across the Atlantic. Youssef was intrigued as well, but doubted the rubber would fare well in the hot climate of his land.

Once the cyclist pedaled off (to the obvious relief of the guards), we continued along the roadway, past butcher shops, farriers, pottery makers, and wood carvers as well as the small neat homes so typical of Upper Genoa. The Imam and her people continually expressed amazement at the greenness of their surroundings, lush with small flower and vegetable gardens, and shaded parks. Matteo explained the ancient custom of dedicating areas to plant growth as part of the continuing effort to restore the natural environment of Italy so sadly damaged in the Terrible Ages. Doctor Braam, who had accompanied us, added such plantings helped glorify God's creation of which we are a part and cannot separate ourselves from without courting disaster. The Imam nodded, answering her people had come to a similar conclusion and were making attempts of their own to restore the natural grandeur of the Nile.

We chanced to pause in front of a printer's shop as Ricardio needed to sit, his weak leg beginning to pain him from so much walking. The owner of the shop had hung out a number of printed pages for display to passersby which instantly drew the attention of the Imam. She fingered the paper and touched the print, murmuring in astonishment over the clarity and consistency of the writing. We explained this was the result of the printing process. When it was apparent she did not understand what we meant, I called to the shop owner who was peering out at us, asking if he would give a demonstration of printing. This he was clearly delighted to do.

The shop owner, one Ousmane Sanchez, proudly showed off his printing presses, of which he had three, one an extremely expensive New Bostonian press he had managed to acquire several years ago. The others were locally produced thanks to the New Bostonians who, on discovering that most Europeans had lost this critical technology, helpfully included design specifications for their production and maintenance along with each press they sold (much to the impotent fury of the Reichers). With the assistance of his Genoan wife and numerous children, he proceeded to demonstrate the inking of the press plates and insertion of paper. After a turn of the print screw, he slid the drawer with the paper back out. Carefully peeling it off, he displayed the fully printed page to the Imam, who stared at it stunned speechless for the first time since her arrival. When she recovered herself, she turned to us with tears in her eyes and began speaking for the first time in Old English, her voice quavering with emotion.

Now it was clear to her how much her people had truly lost in the Age of Suffering and how far they had to go before they could even begin to equal the little we had. Their struggles preserving the tattered pieces of knowledge they possessed, in the midst of a ruined land filled with industrial relics from a millennium before, had been bitter. The ancient pyramids, which had somehow avoided the destruction during those times, were the only things that had kept their ancestors from completely despairing, and through the centuries served as a reminder of an earlier shining greatness that might be again. The reflooding of the Nile and the renewed fertility that came with it brought hope, but how to build on it? How to deal with the sicknesses which often happened when ancient trash heaps were uncovered? How to ensure consistently good crops and healthy children? We are like confused ants (I try to quote her very words here, Aiden) wandering about inside the house of a long dead giant vast beyond imagining unable to comprehend what we see or how to make use of it. Will we ever have hope of becoming giants ourselves? We wish to avoid the mistakes of our ancestors which nearly led to their complete destruction, but how can we do that if we have forgotten how those mistakes came about or even what they were? This is why we search for knowledge.

By the time she finished speaking, those of us who knew Old English were unashamedly weeping, for we all understood her anguish. Who among us has not looked upon the surviving relics: the hollowed-out shells of huge aircraft and trains, the corroded hulks of magnificent giant ships, tree-covered massive heaps once glittering skyscrapers, struggling to grasp how they could have been made? How often have we as scholars read the ancient texts of what once existed and wept knowing we would likely never be able to reproduce these wonders. With the petroleum gone, we are once more in the hands of God and must live in harmony with His laws if we wish to prosper and know greatness again as the Egyptians dream of doing.

Taking a deep breath to restore her composure, she gestured for her guards to set down the wooden chest they had so diligently been carrying. Now, not bothering to use Youssef for translation, she explained their trading occasionally brought curiosities, the origins uncertain to her but now that she had seen the maps we had, she realized they likely came from places far beyond the borders they knew. If we could identify where the contents of the chest came from, it might be possible for her people to eventually make contact and reestablish the ancient trade routes for all our benefit, not just that of the Egyptians. She drew a key out from within her robe and opened the chest. At once a marvelous aroma flooded the room.

Within the chest was a bolt of cloth along with what appeared to be shavings of bark. She lifted the cloth to display it. Bright yellow, it shimmered with a wonderful luster. At first I thought it to be an ancient synthetic cloth but it was too fresh and new in appearance to be that. Matteo gasped and identified it before the rest of us could. Silk!

Yes, Aiden, there could be little doubt it was silk, the craft of making it lost centuries ago to us. We gently handled it, delighting in its softness and the delicate pattern of flowers imprinted into it. How had the Imam come by it, we asked? She could only say that it had been part of a gift to the Caliph from the leader of some Ymani nomads who lived in the area near the Meccan ruins. How they acquired it, she knew not, but said they often wandered about the old Saudi lands trading with other nomadic tribes of that region and likely obtained it from one of them. Where it came from before that, no one could guess. With the permission of the Caliph, she had brought it on their voyage in the hopes of attracting trade contacts.

While we avidly discussed the sources of silk in olden times and how this particular bolt of cloth might have arrived on the Arabian peninsula, Doctor Braam darted forward and knelt beside the chest. It was not the cloth which captured his attention but the reddish brown bark shavings. He sniffed them intently, even breaking off a small piece and tasting it. Sanchez's children gathered around, squealing with delight at the wonderful scent when he offered it to them for a sniff. He looked up hopefully at the Imam and asked if it was cinnamon. The old lady, sensing she had scored a coup, nodded with a smile.

Spices and silk, Aiden! As you can imagine, this swirled around in our minds, during the rest of the tour we gave the Imam. She in her turn could think of nothing but the printing press she had seen, and the wonderful possibilities it unfolded in her mind, as she confessed to me later on. If the only thing she brought back to Egypt was the design for building one, she could rest content in her old age, knowing she had given her people a vital tool in rebuilding their civilization and restoring the learning they hungered for.

But of course that is not the only thing she will bring back. Several Essenes will accompany her to Egypt, the goal being to re-establish the trade not just in cinnamon but in frankincense and myrrh along with other herbs unobtainable in Europe both for medicines and perfumes. Youssef and his sister have their herbs from the Essene hospital to take home and the governor gave several olive tree saplings to the Imam. I obtained a large copy of an atlas and offered it to her as a gift, while she in exchange presented me with a hand written copy of the Quran made of papyrus, its cover painted with exquisitely elegant geometric designs enclosing images of the pyramids and inlaid with thin strips of gold. A fine acquisition for the Vatican Archives! When they left after a nearly three week stay, they were escorted by two well-armed Piedmont ships, to guard against piracy on their long journey home.

As for the silk, the Imam allowed us to keep a small portion of it. I and Matteo believe it most likely made its way from India, which means commerce has reappeared in that land and certainly others as well. Time will tell of course. You no doubt immediately noticed when you opened my letter that I included fragments of cinnamon. I hope you enjoy the aroma as much as I do. It isn't generally known but the Archives actually contain copies of ancient cook books, preserved no doubt by someone who liked their food! I find myself reading and wondering about the ingredients in the recipes, some quite mysterious to me. What is lemon grass? Or turmeric? Even pepper was lost to us, when the Terrible Ages brought everything down in a crashing heap. Now we must begin again. I pray with God's help, we shall do better this time and honor His creation by always enhancing the beauty of the world, not devouring it like so many locusts as our ancestors did.

I look forward to your next letter, Aiden. May God's peace be ever with you.

Cardinal Dominic Benenati
Senior Archivist

THE TOXICITY OF WATER

BY RALPH WALKER

EVERYTHING WAS DAMP AGAIN. Nothing had soaked all the way through, but the wet parts would bloom into mold or worse if he let it go. He pressed a dry sponge against the base of the wooden toolbox, soaking up what he could. The color faded a shade with each pass. Inside the open top, the Ziploc seals were tight, but the metal had gouged the bags too many times. Moisture would get in again soon.

"Is there any more saran, Dot?"

"Not for metal, Sherman," she called back. "I need it for the cheese, and the herbs."

"We shouldn't preserve them if they don't have any flavor left." He said it loud enough she might hear him, if she bothered to listen. It was an old fight. She wanted to save the basil and the tarragon. He wanted to save the Philips heads and the Allen keys. They were both right.

Sherman left the tool box in a slice of sunlight and shuffled back across the deck of loose pallets to the main house. It pained him to use that word to describe their dwelling, but the stand of tent poles he had lashed together was working pretty well and, since the truck bed sat high over the wheels, their home was cramped but dry. Dot had rolled back their quilted roof of tarps to let things air out for the afternoon. The potted plants were doing fine on the ground, but he needed a better place for his toolbox. Once the rain returned, he couldn't leave the metals out in the elements. All too soon they'd surely rust.

Maybe he shouldn't be concerned. They'd have to be moving along again before too long, looking for higher ground. No matter what Dot thought they couldn't resettle, not here. It wouldn't matter if the rains came or not.

Sherman climbed onto the steel bumper and sat on what used to be his old nightstand. King James was still stuffed in the top drawer along with his will and a

Smith & Wesson he had never learned to shoot. He pulled off his boots and socks and dropped them onto the welcome mat Dot had grabbed in the panic. He pulled a dirty towel off the igloo cooler and dried his feet. The wrinkles of age and wet were impossible to discern.

Dot worked a roux, shaking flour over the shallow pan. He rose up and paused at her shoulder. "How much do we have left?"

"Enough to have a decent meal with your grandson." She worked the shredded bacon in between the cattails and cabbage. From the bite in her voice Sherman knew they wouldn't need any pepper, at least not tonight.

"I don't like him coming here," he said.

"Why, because you are embarrassed? This will be his someday, too. Besides, it isn't your choice. I invited him."

Sherman grumbled as he crossed the flatbed and sat on a dining room chair to rub his corns. Dead skin peeled under his thumb. The itch felt good.

Hunter climbed over the third felled tree and got back on the asphalt. He strode up Rose Glen Road alongside the guardrail. The tree's shadows were long but the sky was still a day tone of blue. He arrived at the makeshift deck: a dozen wooden pallets fitted together, littered with potted vegetables, an unlit lantern, and Sherman's wooden toolbox. Two plastic deckchairs waited, vacant in the center. The truck was parked on the uphill side, straddling a wet stone gutter, the cab dark but the curved plastic roof glowing. Slices of lantern light poked out between the outer wall of bookshelves and dressers. He could hear the action inside.

The fry pan sizzled and popped while Dorothy stirred. A metal canister snapped like a snare drum as Sherman dropped in hardware and plucked it back out again. Hunter ducked his head under the tarp.

"Hi Nana." The boy's smile was wide as he hopped up to the bumper. The flat bed tow truck had been a blessing. Solid engine, high wheelbase, large bed, it had mostly kept them out of the wet and made it easy to move, but there really wasn't enough room to bring everything. They had a little extra elbow room when they could make camp and spread out.

He dumped his deflated dry pack next to their boots. She put down the spoon and wrapped an arm around her kin's neck, kissing him on the cheek from behind. "I have an extra pair for you." She pulled a knot of frayed white athletic socks from the leg pocket of her over-worn fatigues.

Hunter smiled over his shoulder. "Thanks Nana, but I brought my own." His skinny arm held up a pair of grey woolies. He dried his feet and donned the socks.

Hunter half stood, half crouched under the arched tarp and picked his way toward the dining table that dominated the flatbed. Careful to stay on the knotted carpet, he ducked under mason jars hanging from the bents and high stepped over plastic milk crates on the floor. Sherman kept every version of grinder and screwdriver and bow saw he could find. Hunter wasn't sure what he was saving the hand tools for, but he seemed to have one of every type should some need arise.

"How far have the waters receded?" Sherman never waited to ask the most important question.

"Not far enough." Hunter stretched out a hand to his grandfather and the smaller man shook it, then pulled the boy in for an awkward embrace. The kid had grown long, like his mother. His features were flat: ears pressed back, hands like paddles, too thin around the middle. Dot always tried to ply him with scrapple or pork roll when they could get it, but he always pushed it back to them. He never did eat enough meat.

"Not far enough," Sherman echoed as he let the boy go. "Where are you working?"

Hunter straddled a crate with a pillow top and pulled up to the dining table that doubled as Dorothy and Sherman's bed. "Got a dive gig out of Pennsauken. They've taken half a dozen of us."

"Dive gig?" Dot smiled back. "Sounds like you'll need seconds."

"Based on what I smell, I might need thirds."

The meal didn't last long. Dot stretched the bacon and cattails as far as they would go. Everyone ate enough. After plates were cleaned, Sherman fished a gallon jug out from behind his chair. He poured three shots of cloudy clear into Dot's favorite teacups and passed them around.

Dot raised her cup to her nose and let the moonshine touch her lips. She smiled adoringly at her husband and pushed the cup to her grandson. "You need the hair on your chest more than me."

Hunter, mid-sip on his own drink, almost spit at his grandmother's statement. "I'm not fifteen anymore Nana. I'm pretty well done growing."

"I hope so, or I'm going to have to raid some highlander's pantry before you visit anymore." She reached across and mussed his hair.

Sherman sipped his drink. Hunter slowed himself down, watching the older man. The space heater splashed a warm orange light across the plastic and hung glass. Their shadows danced on the checkerboard tablecloth.

"I'm working on the peninsula." Hunter watched his grandfather's face.

"Oh?" He took another sip. "North end?"

"No. The Schuylkill."

Sherman's eyes found Dot's. He tipped back his teacup, finished his drink and folded his hands. "Are they diving the west side of Philly again? We heard the water has been too fast."

"They've been dropping temporary eddies. The water is shallower too, not receded, not yet, but shallower. Besides, north Philly has been picked over," Hunter said.

"You best be careful." Sherman frowned. "Those temporary eddies just make the water go faster, other side of the structures."

"I know, Grandpop." Hunter's lips flattened.

"Do you think you'll be going down Twenty-Fourth Street?" Dot asked.

"They have to do the whole city, Dorothy. Don't get your hopes up. Every block is swamped."

"They showed us new maps today. Rooflines are emerging for some two story buildings north of Grey's Ferry. Tidal water isn't getting past Reed Street anymore. Everything is still swamped, but it's a pool, not a river." Hunter focused on his grandmother. "I don't know what there will be to recover, but I have to go down Twenty-Fourth Street each way. It can't hurt to look."

Sherman muttered under his breath.

"It is as much his as ours." Dot's eyes were on her husband.

Sherman licked his top lip, feeling the chapped skin. "Diving a wreck isn't anything like salvage. You'll do more damage than good. You should wait for the waters to drop."

Hunter expected this argument. "And if they never recede? I can't do anything if there's nothing left to salvage."

"So why go? The buildings are surely unstable. The water might be toxic. Don't put yourself at risk. You are more important to us than anything else." Sherman flipped his teacup upside down.

"Because some salvager is going to get in there sooner or later. We both know it's better if it's me. Besides, I know what to look for." Their grandson stood up and gathered his dry bag from the rear of the truck. He pinched the compressor seal, letting the bright orange rubber expand with new air. Reaching inside, he pulled out a rolled towel, still damp. Tenderly he unrolled the cloth across the table and motioned to his grandmother. She leaned in close to see. Dozens of large seeds were revealed.

She picked at a seed with a crooked finger. "Pumpkin?" she asked hopefully.

Hunter nodded. "We found them two days ago. There was a bushel that hadn't burst. We each took one."

She silently counted the seeds. "Those are worth—"

"They aren't worth anything if you can't plant them," Hunter interrupted. "I figured you'd know what to do with them better than most." He turned back to his grandfather. "The pilots think the water rose calmly on some streets. When the sea wall broke the river's inflow balanced against the tide somewhere around Passyunk.

Most of Center City is probably a big swimming pool."

"Doesn't mean anything survived. There are only six steps from the kitchen to the street."

"I should still look."

Dot rinsed the plates, stowing them in the nightstand. Sherman folded up the table leaf, widening the surface so he could lay with his wife in their bed, such as it was. Hunter walked with the lantern and tucked down the hem of the tarps outside. Sherman finished and hopped down from the truck bed to the deck in bare feet.

"They say the rain is coming hard next week," Hunter said.

Sherman nodded.

"Are you going to stay here?" Hunter asked.

Sherman looked back at Dot, finishing with the dishes, then out to the woods, and then down the road to the felled trees. A few electric lights tried to peak through the foliage. "She'd like to, but we can't stay long. We did a good job, but someone is going to clear those trees eventually."

Hunter looked back to his grandmother. She was sitting close to the lantern now, counting the seeds again. The two men moved towards the edge of camp. Hunter clasped his grandfather's shoulder. "Don't go far."

"We won't. If we go, you'll find us on higher ground. We'll leave our mark." He put out his hand for a shake.

Hunter felt the metal pushed into his palm.

Sherman leaned close. "Your grandmother is right. It is as much yours as ours. Be careful."

The next morning Hunter traversed a cable bridge to the I-676 platform. The on-ramps had all washed away, but there was more than a half mile of elevated concrete road that remained stable. Private salvage crews had set up to work off the platform. A dozen slips and a pair of small cranes were enough to handle their operation.

Three flat boats were still docked. Hunter found the same group of divers he had worked with all week. All twelve had their wet gear on, and empty dry bags at their feet. They just needed a ride. Moesha and Roy huddled with some of the others guessing how much treasure they might find today. Pale Simon had his back turned to the group, staring at the water, wringing his hands. Hunter lingered outside the circle.

A brunette in a ball cap and jeans crossed the platform, unhooked a chain at one of the pseudo gangplanks and motioned to Roy. The divers all climbed onto the steel hulled salvager, each finding a spot on the bench. Hunter got on last and the brunette, Tesso, followed marching back to the open cabin. She started the gas engine and let it rumble while she stalked the deck, checking hoses, compressors and the winch. Her face hid behind oversized sunglasses. She didn't make eye contact with any of the divers. She threw off the bow rope and pushed the boat out from the slip, before returning to the captain's chair.

Hunter stared at the river. They were floating fast along with the brown blue water. He couldn't see bottom.

Without warning, Tesso turned the wheel and gunned the throttle. Hunter reached for the steel bench, but couldn't stop himself from slamming into Roy, the muscle bound diver next to him. Moesha, in her three point subway stance, snickered at him from across the way.

"Sorry."

Roy shrugged it off.

Moesha was still laughing. Hunter turned to her and shouted over the engine. "Do you know how many streets we're doing today?" She wore the same hot pink tiger stripe swim shirt he had seen her in the last five dives. Her flippers were cut short and tipped with neon green electrical tape. On their first dive together she had joked it was the closest thing she'd had to a pedicure since the waters rose.

"Panama, Pine, Waverly, maybe Lombard," she shouted back.

"That's it?"

She looked at him sideways while she wrapped her spool. "We aren't making it to South Street yet."

"I don't care about South Street."

She squeezed up her face and looked at Roy. "He doesn't care about South Street. I told you this kid is a tourist."

Roy considered Hunter again.

"I'm in this for more than money."

Moesha raised her eyebrow. "Oh? You're a Samaritan, huh? If you want to drop concrete boxes or pull bodies the Feds are looking for volunteers. They could use a nice boy like you. You could swim down and try to find some of those babies still strapped into their car seats. You look like the kind who wants to be a hero."

Hunter had heard the story. A diver had found two twins still strapped in. The driver had crashed and drown, but the minivan floated. One baby survived, sucking on a pocket of air. The other—Hunter shivered. "I'm no Samaritan." He wasn't a hero, either.

"Good, 'cause I don't got time for that. We need to get our shit done so we can get to South Street. That's where the money is at." Moesha spat.

The chop calmed as they passed between two apartment buildings, each kneeling in the muddy water. Hunter said a silent prayer as they entered the city of brotherly love.

‡‡

The early dives were short. There was barely anything worth salvaging on Panama or Pine. The boat bottom was littered with sealed bottles of motor oil, scrap metal and garden hoses. Hunter grabbed some faucets and a shower head. One of the others found a wallet and a few dollars cash, still dry in a Ziploc. Tesso made him give her the cash and throw back the leather. No one was getting rich today. They would barely cover fuel costs.

Waverly had been a different story. They found a firetruck and an ambulance submerged under a collapsed building. The truck had been marked on the salvage maps a full block away, but it must have drifted. Underwater it was impossible to tell if the building had fallen violently from the impact or crumpled over in slow motion. Either way, the brick had heaped on the truck. Most of the divers worked the ladder truck. Hunter followed Moesha and Simon to the ambulance.

"I got an air pocket in the back," Simon called out over the two way.

Hunter swam down to find the hatch open. The gurney was gone. Most of the cabinets hung open. A pyramid of stale air was trapped in the top. Simon's torso was above the water line stuffing medical supplies into his dry bag. Hunter stayed below and grabbed at anything that looked like it might survive.

Moesha swam in. "You leave anything for me, crabs?"

"Closest to the door," Simon said, pointing back into the water towards the defibrillator and the ready kits.

"Shorted out batteries and water logged gauze? Gee thanks." She grabbed the bags anyway.

One by one the divers surfaced, chucking cinched orange dry-bags and loose hunks of metal over the side of the skiff.

"Anything worthwhile in the truck?" Moesha asked, still treading water.

"Some meds and parts. Roy got the best stuff."

The barrel chested black man was already aboard. He held a massive tool over his head and smiled. "The Jaws of Life!" He flipped a switch and the combo tool started right up. It looked brand new. "Air pockets in the upper cabinets. Everything was dry."

Moesha pushed off. "I've got air left. I'll go back down." She wasn't one to leave a cache for someone else.

"No!" Hunter said it too quick.

"I want to get paid off that truck. We should go back down." Moesha looked at Tesso.

An oversized air bubble rose and popped on the port side of the boat. Simon stared at it. "Somebody left a door open. Things are shifting."

Tesso logged what they had pulled up on her clipboard. "We got enough. Get on board, Moesha. Nobody is swimming home."

A pair of cut flippers with green electrical tape flew over the side.

Tesso stopped in front of Hunter. "You know something?"

"No. I just want to get further south."

"Everybody wants to get to South Street," Simon said, parroting Moesha.

Back onto the boat, she shook off the water and shot a middle finger at Simon. "He doesn't care about South Street. He's not in it for the money. He's some fucking Samaritan."

Tesso ignored the wet tigress. "Where?"

Hunter felt her gaze. He looked at the other divers. No one was here for sentimental reasons. They all had families to feed or debts to pay. Everyone had lost something. At the same time, with the take from the fire truck, they had already made money. The sun was high enough in the sky. There was still gas in the engine.

"Twenty-Fourth Street."

"Twenty-Fourth and what?" Tesso didn't budge.

"Naudain." Hunter regretted it as soon as he gave it breath.

"Oh come on, kid," Roy said. That's a waste of air."

Tesso pulled her cap down and returned to the cabin. She put a foot up against the wheel and pulled out her charts, letting them drift while the divers hashed it out.

"What's so special about Twenty-Fourth and Naudain?" Simon asked.

"Nothing," Moesha snapped. "It isn't South Street."

Hunter looked at Simon and doubled down. "The feds cleared it early, but no one has picked it over yet, not once since the flood."

"You think there's something worth finding there?" Simon asked.

"It doesn't matter. The river blew it out. You've seen the maps—those streets got power washed. There isn't going to be anything worth looking for," Moesha said.

"I don't think so. When the Atlantic charged up the rivers and the water turned back into the city some of the streets were sluiceways, but not all. Sure Penrose, Passyunk, Oregon got punched in the mouth, but they run east-west."

"So?"

"Twenty-Fourth Street runs north-south. We've all seen it. Some streets are underwater, but barely have any damage at all. The water came up slower, calmer in a few places. I think it's worth a look."

"There was nothing there worth saving before the rise," Moesha said.

Hunter swallowed the sting. "Maybe not in the stores, but there were wealthy people living in the apartments. They must have had silver, brass, maybe some jewelry?"

"I'm not dry-walking. Anything above the high water line is still stealing," Roy piped up.

Another burp of large bubbles popped next to the boat.

Roy was right. They couldn't ransack dry floors, but Hunter didn't need anything above the second story. Dot and Sherman's colonial had fully flooded. Only the attic and roof deck remained dry in the surge. Last week's flyover pictures gave Hunter hope.

Tesso swiveled back on her chair and called from the cabin. "How much did you get so far?"

Hunter rifled through his dry bag. "Eight prescription bottles, an Epi-Pen, two IV bags, a couple of faucets, some copper pipe. Enough."

She nodded at Roy. "And you got your toys?"

He nodded back.

She got out of her chair and walked the deck, scanning the rest of the divers. "Everybody is already getting paid today." The divers all nodded. She stopped in front of Hunter. "You know something about this block."

"I do."

"You want to go so bad. Give it up."

Hunter swallowed. "That section of Naudian is a pretty rich block. I used to help people out in that neighborhood, handyman type stuff. Seemed like any other block, but everyone was a little richer: nice watches, jewelry, collectables. Everyone paid in cash. I know at least one guy kept his valuables in a floor safe, the watertight kind." Enough was true that he kept the whole boat's attention.

"How would you know about the safe?" Simon asked.

"I put it in, between the floor joists."

"When you were fifteen?"

"Twelve. My Dad was the one they hired. He could build just about anything. I tagged along and helped out."

"A floor safe sounds promising." Moesha pulled a map up on the dive tablet.

"Might be enough for one, but I got a boat full of divers. What else is there Hunter?" Tesso wasn't convinced.

"There are two banks on the block."

"ATMs are a waste of time. Too much work to salvage and the parts are worth less than the cash inside," Roy said.

Hunter had played his last card. If his story wasn't enough they would surely skip the block today, maybe altogether.

"Pawn shop!" Moesha called out. "Sign said 'Diamond Broker' too."

Hunter encouraged her. "The owners had an apartment on the block. They weren't going anywhere."

Roy smiled. "Hard goods. I can get behind that."

Simon leaned across Moesha to Hunter. "I thought you said this was a rich block?"

Moesha slapped Simon on the cheek playfully. "Some people are rich in ways you just wouldn't understand."

Tesso turned back to the cabin. "Sounds like we have a winner. We only have an hour to dive. Everybody in?" She started the engine back up, not bothering to wait for an answer. The flat boat cut a hard turn, sending a foamy wake in all directions.

Hunter lost his balance and reached for the rail. He missed and grabbed Moesha's arm instead.

"Don't go getting fresh. You got your dive."

Hunter's eyes widened. He slid back to his place.

Moesha's face softened, flashing a stark white smile against her coffee face. "Tell me about that safe."

"Second floor, under a four poster bed."

"Am I gonna find your baby pictures in it?"

Hunter looked at her in disbelief.

She turned the tablet so he could see it. A search page for the phone book was open next to the map. "Ceppelli, right?"

There was no denying it. His name was printed in black on his dry bag and the leg of his wetsuit.

"This is your parent's house?"

"Grandparents. Don't tell."

"There ain't nothing to tell. I'm not looking for heirlooms. I'm in this for the good stuff." Her finger was on the corner building with Mr. Hiltor's pawn shop. "Diamonds, right?"

Hunter nodded.

"Perpendicular current," Simon yelled over the motor. "Top water is running eight miles an hour west to east. There might be an undertow. This is real close to the confluence between the Schuykill and the Atlantic."

"So this is a waste of time. Nothing should be standing," Roy said.

"The roofs are still there. It could be a lagoon. Maybe the currents balanced each other out." Hunter had been thinking about this for days.

Simon shook his head. "Wishful thinking. If the pressure somehow balanced, I'd bet as soon as somebody pops a window the whole place comes down. There is no way this section is stable."

"So stay on the boat if you don't have the stones to dive, Simon," Moesha dared. "All of Philly is unstable."

The engine quieted.

"Gear up," Tesso commanded. "We're here."

Barely a floor of the old colonials peaked above the water line. Skirts of broken branches gathered high around the trunks of street trees. One flat roof was piled with crates and suitcases. More than half had been opened and rifled through by weather or wanderer, or most likely wind. A dress fluttered in the breeze, its hanger caught on a roof gutter. It was the same as almost every other street Hunter had seen, but that was his grandparent's house. That was his mother's dress.

"The pawnshop was there on the first floor." He pointed southwest, the opposite corner from the fluttering polka dots. "The valuable stuff is either in the basement or the second floor. I'd check both."

"Are you sure?" Roy asked.

He looked back at his fellow divers. *Sure you aren't going to find anything of value*, he thought. Mr. Hiltor only ever dealt in rhinestones, digital watches and pop guns. "Pretty sure. Look for the blacked out windows." Hunter needed the time. He started to ready his gear.

Moesha was already ready to dive. She had washed out the filter on her rebreather and cleared her snorkel. Two orange dry bags were knotted to her shoulder straps. A finisher's claw hung from her belt and a shiny set of pointed brass knuckles weighed down her unwebbed hand. She smiled at Hunter as if she might eat him for lunch and shouted, "Smash and grab, right?"

He shrugged on his own kit and knotted the bags at his waist. "Yeah, smash and grab."

Simon was kneeling over the rail, fingers in the water. He stared at the water surface, trying to read the currents. "You see that?" Two blocks down, a peaked slate roof floated by, chimney and all. Simon counted out loud as it passed. "Top water has to be going at least ten miles an hour."

None of the divers paid much attention when Simon got like this. His head spun around looking from face to face for someone else to reinforce his anxiety.

"Tesso?"

"What Simon?"

"Are we moving? I mean do you have the engine going? You are pushing against the current to keep us in one place, right?"

Tesso stepped away from the Captain's chair, putting her hands halfway up. "Do you hear anything?" The ignition key hung from her fingers in plain sight. The whole boat was still, floating midblock, barely a ripple in the water. "Are you getting wet?"

Simon looked past the key at the islands of brick and shingles, resting in still water. "Where is the stake?"

Moesha pointed to the low rise brick building that marked the corner. "You better hurry if you think I'm going to share any of those diamonds."

Simon's eyes followed the ridge of water that crossed just beyond the face of the target building. "The confluence between fast and slow water is the most unstable part of the current. You don't know what you'll find."

"Exactly, so go find something. You've got fifty minutes. Simon, if you don't dive you can swim back. We'll go to South Street on our own." Tesso restarted the engine.

Hunter leaned into Simon. "Stay north of the intersection. The whole thing is an eddy. Calm waters." He pulled on his mask.

"No such thing as calm. Held back, or contained maybe, but it's just waiting to flow." Simon pulled his filter and cleared it.

Six divers flipped over the side in unison. The first four swam straight for the corner, but the other two didn't rush. Hunter sank straight down under the boat, wanting to put space between him and the rest of them. Simon was just a slow coward.

Hunter fell all the way to the street before turning on his headlamp. The street looked mostly clear, almost clean. The postbox was still mounted to the sidewalk. Doors were still on their hinges. The windows weren't even broken. It was eerie swimming here. It was as if someone had turned on all the bathtubs on the block, and let them run forever. Stuff that floated found its way out, but anything bolted down had stayed in place.

Hunter started for number eighty-eight, following the path he would have taken from the bus. It was weird to swim instead of walk. The nylon straps of his diving gear cut into his shoulders the same as his old backpack, weighed down with school books, used to. Tiny bits of his old life swirled about. His headlamp caught scraps churned up when the waters rose: plastic shopping bags, a broken child's car, the cover of a smoke alarm. The rest had fallen, collecting in the corners like piles of leaves in the fall, caught between stoops.

"Six on the pawn shop." The crackle startled him. No one communicated much at the start of a dive. Everyone was looking for their own stake before they helped out the rest of the boat.

Six steps up, the black door with its brass knocker looked unharmed. Hunter rolled down the waistband of his wetsuit and pulled out a single key. His grandfather had never trusted anyone with that key before, just like his father had never trusted anyone with the keys to his truck. The stamped brass slid into the deadbolt and turned with a jiggle. Kicking his feet, Hunter pushed open the door.

Between the swelling and the rug the door only cracked open eighteen inches before locking in place. He could have popped the hinges or busted the frame, but that was a last resort. Hunter unstrapped his rebreather and pushed it through in front of him as he swam in the house. He didn't even bother unclipping his spool. He knew his way around.

The living room looked as if someone had picked it up and dropped it. The brown leather couch Sherman loved to nap on was cracked and swollen in a corner.

Stacks of beloved books and magazines were nothing more than wet rags. Somehow the pictures had stayed on the walls. Hunter kept moving.

Nana's kitchen was mostly cleaned out. She was the one who had insisted they leave. Sherman had called her a busy body, but she was always plugged in. The under counter monitor was still hanging over the stove, splattered with grease. She loved watching the feeds while she cooked, keeping up on the latest murder investigation or crime report. Every Thanksgiving she made an extra apple crumb cake to walk down to the firehouse. As he got bigger she made Hunter carry it for her, and she introduced him to each of the "Heroes of Engine Company Nine."

Maybe she was being overdramatic, but she had started packing before the water mounted the first step. They had been lucky the flatbed started that day. Sherman only had it to replace the fuel pump for Dad the night before. He never did finish fixing the radio.

"Twenty minutes. Status report." Tesso was in his ear.

"Four cleaning out the pawn shop. Roy and I are scouting for the diamonds. Basement is mostly collapsed. I don't think Ceppelli had it right," Moesha said, more for Hunter than Tesso.

"Hunter?" Tesso scolded through the static.

"Did they clean out the second floor? Try the apartments next door. I think they owned those too." He wanted more time.

"Where are you?" Moesha asked.

Hunter swam up the stairs.

"Who has eyes on Ceppelli?" Moesha asked.

"He's midblock. There's a door cracked. Number eighty-eight," Simon said.

"Are you with him?" Tesso asked.

"No. My spool got caught up. I'm outside."

"Safety first, Simon. Safety first," Moesha taunted. "I'm coming to you."

The door to his grandparent's bedroom wouldn't budge. Sherman must have closed it tight before they left. Now swollen, the opening was the strongest part of the wall. Hunter swam into the adjacent room, his father's childhood bedroom, and found the closet. Closet walls were always the thinnest in these old colonials. He remembered listening through the walls while his mother searched for him on the other side as they played hide and seek. He pulled a drywall knife from the sheaf at his leg. The jagged blade made short work of the wall board, leaving a hole between the studs just large enough.

The bedroom was a disaster. Small unrecognizable bits of his grandparent's old life swirled around. Once they had decided to leave, Dorothy hadn't worried about the state of affairs they left behind.

Hunter swallowed hard. He wished his parents had heeded the same warnings.

He pushed the waterlogged mattress and frame up and over. The safe was recessed in the hardwood floor, fully exposed. The false floorboards had floated out of place. Hunter knelt, focusing his light on the dial: eleven, six, fifty-four. Sherman always used his wedding anniversary for the combination, said it was the only way he could remember. Hunter wasn't sure if he meant the combination or the anniversary.

The dry safe door popped open and a gasp of air bubbles escaped around Hunter's face. Grey-brown water flooded in. A stack of papers almost as old as his family immediately began to disintegrate. Ink divorced from pulp. Paper curled over on itself. Hunter grabbed what he could, trying to stuff the birth certificates and deeds, and wedding licenses into the dry bag. They were lost, his family's paper history washed away in still water. A few trinkets lay in the bottom: a pair of medals from Sherman's father's army service, a short string of pearls, an opal ring, a dozen coins from some other shore. Hunter stuffed them all in, wishing he didn't have to claim his inheritance this way.

A light crossed the room.

"There you are," Hunter heard Moesha in his ear. She was floating outside the bedroom window along with Simon and Roy. "Find your baby pictures?"

Hunter didn't wait. He cinched the bag shut and swam for the closet. He ran the compressor as he moved, caving the rubber in on itself, tight to its contents. There was one more thing he needed.

Moesha smashed the glass with her brass knuckle, getting inside in an instant. Ray ripped the hinges off the bedroom door, while Moesha cut the frame. Hunter was already up the stairs when they broke through.

Water topped out a foot above the last step. Hunter splashed out, feeling the weight of his gear. The attic was the hardest. His parents had moved up there after Dad's job was gone. Hunter couldn't linger over the four poster bed tucked under the dormer. He went straight to the deck.

The screen door was off its hinges. Muddy water splashed around his knees. Outside, he pulled up his mask, catching his breath. Cushions floated, trapped inside the railing. The metal chairs were long gone. Across the submerged courtyard, a row of five roof decks all poked out, just like the one he stood on. He remembered playing in the yards below, under a canopy of strung up laundry and chattering neighbors, calling across the rooftops. His mother used to sit up here and talk with his grandmother while he scampered about below.

Trapped between the row houses, the water was still.

The pots were still there!

Moesha crashed outside. "Why are you up here? What are you doing? Taking in the view? If you're done diving get back to the boat. You are going to lose your stake if you keep this shit up."

Hunter kneeled in the water and looked under the leaves. The fruit was plump and purple and red. A few had already burst, but at least six looked healthy. He unzipped his wetsuit and pulled a hand towel from his breast.

Moesha looked over his shoulder. "Tomatoes? You came out here for tomatoes? What was in the safe, Hunter?"

He plucked a fist sized tomato from the stem and cradled it in his palm. "My inheritance." He wrapped the fruit and placed it tenderly in a dry bag. "These are Morados, my family's heirlooms. Do you want one? More are ripe on the vine than I can carry."

"I don't want one of your goddamn tomatoes! Tomatoes don't pay the bills. Where is the jewelry, the cash, the diamonds? This your house, your neighborhood. Where are the fucking valuables?"

The water started to ripple. Hunter held out a second tomato to Moesha.

She shook her head. "There isn't anything here, is there?"

"Here, take one. It's the last of their kind. There aren't any more like them."

The house started to shift. Simon emerged from the attic, his spool unwinding behind him. Ray followed, untethered.

"The structure is breaking," Simon called out. His head turned on a swivel, barely holding back panic as he looked for an escape route.

Ray still had his mask on. "Tesso will bring the boat to us."

"Where is she?" Simon asked.

Hunter pointed to the main roof. Simon and Ray didn't wait, pulling themselves up and over, back towards the street.

"The pawn shop just collapsed," Simon called back, now in full panic. "We have to go."

Moesha took a tomato, stowing it in her bag and gave Hunter a look. "Last of their kind?"

He nodded.

They both climbed onto the roof. Moesha followed the others, sliding down and splashing into the water. Hunter paused, straddling the peak of the roof. A turbulent boil swirled where the pawn shop used to be. Half the divers were in the boat. Simon was swimming frantically with Roy and Moesha behind. All three were being pulled in the fast water. The current had shifted. The confluence of river and ocean had moved. Tesso gunned the engines, pointing towards them.

The house groaned and Simon shifted his feet. One flipper went through the shingles. Hunter looked down through the rafters, seeing his parent's bed below.

If only they had listened.

He kneeled to pull himself out. Instead of rising up, he pushed the whole house down. The frame moved and twisted, crumbling under him. He felt heavy, dense, weighed down by loss.

Water bubbled below, first pushing up the mattress, then drowning it under its own weight. The room they slept in flooded. He felt the rafters sink away and him with it.

He hadn't moved, but the house collapsed underneath him. He wasn't standing or swimming or sinking. Hunter bobbed in the water, letting it pull him where it may.

Water splashed his face. The noise got louder. Was it the river or the ocean? It didn't matter. The brine was toxic. It was trying to wash his whole family away.

He heard the roar of the engine before he saw the arms reaching out for him. A hot pink tiger stripe took him by the collar.

The trees had been pulled to the side of the road. Broad sweeping strokes painted the asphalt in mud and dead leaves. The tracks weren't wide but there were more of them than he expected.

As he strode up the hill, Hunter could see the broken wood. Three pallets were splintered into the mud where the rear tires should be. A splash of congealed grease marked the ground where Dot dumped the pan fat. Maybe they left in a hurry, maybe not. Didn't matter. Sherman never left a note, but had taught his grandson what to look for.

Hunter kept going up the hill, rounding a turn into the park. He saw the mark. Shallow axe strokes carved the trunk, pointing him to the top of the hill.

None of the mud tracks appeared to respect the yellow dividing line. Had someone given chase? Hunter hurried.

Broken asphalt became heavy gravel as he followed the marks off the main road. The trees got closer together. Hunter's footsteps crunched loud inside the park. Another mark pointed him into a thicket. There was no way they had driven the truck through here.

Through the trees the canopy opened up. A pool of sunlight shone down on a patch of turned soil, rich and black. A pot marked each corner of the garden.

Hunter squatted at the edge of his grandmother's handiwork. Even if she hadn't convinced Sherman to stay, she had still planted an anchor. They wouldn't go far.

He opened the dry bag and pulled out a wrapped tomato. The fruit had burst, soaking the towel with its juices, but the important part was still intact. Hunter picked three tiny seeds from the carcass. He found a space between the rows of pumpkin seeds and pressed each one into a soft part of the ground, covering them up. They might not grow tall, but this variety was hearty. They would take.

Behind him, Hunter could hear the distinct snap of metal bolts dropping into metal cans. He stood and turned, seeing an arched quilt of plastic tarps beyond the trees.

The Church of the Green Jesus

by Wilson Bertram

MAYBE YOU SAW IT ON THE WAY HERE? It's easy to miss. It used to be notorious in these parts and lots of people came to see it. Now it's just a small dilapidated building in an overgrown patch of woodland.

How did it start? Who started it? What was it about? There's lots of stories about it, and it's hard to know how much truth there may be in any of them. I've lived around here and been interested in the local stories for a long time, and this is the best sense I can make of it.

Way back in the old times, long ago when this was still America, things became real crazy, even before the Collapse and the War. Maybe the craziness was a cause rather than an effect. I don't know. Any ways, it seems that before the end of the old times, some people were scared that the sea was about to rise and swallow them, or the sun was about to burn them up, or the weather was about to go mad and torment them and destroy their crops by unseasonable floods and droughts. They came here, well above sea level, in a temperate climatic zone to live what they considered to be a more holy life. It's a bit like the story of Noah, but without an ark. Some say that these folk were atheists, some say that they were nature worshipers who hoped to propitiate their angry deities by self-chastisement, ritualized farming and gardening, and blaming their neighbors. Why angry gods would be mollified by this behavior is not explained. Perhaps there was some echo of the Exodus story, with the "good guys" expecting to be "passed over" when their neighbors got whacked. Maybe there had to be a sacrifice, probably blood. Other People's Blood, usually better than Other People's Money for making things happen in such stories. It's difficult to imagine angry gods being satisfied with an offering of fresh vegetables, now isn't it? There is that Cain and Abel precedent.

When the bad times came, everyone got whacked. Some of the "Greenies," as they were known, survived; probably helped by having become proficient kitchen gardeners—and by ceasing to blame their neighbors. This is all background. The real story begins a bit later, after the War, in the Templar Era.

At that point the Greenies were gaining adherents as well as a reputation for being "holier than thou," which other people disliked; especially those other people who considered that they were the more holy ones. The American Inquisition became active, and anything obviously unchristian came under scrutiny. Part of the craziness hanging over from the old times was that some of these Greenies had been known to boast of being wizards, apparently without having the expected skills of being able to turn opponents into green frogs, and so forth. This was remembered against them. At that time one of the most popular Biblical quotes became, "Thou shalt not suffer a witch to live." Some have claimed to discern different shades or colors of witchcraft, but to the popular mind, and to religious orthodoxy, it's all black. Some of them became air pollution and cinders, a particularly sad fate for those reputed to have abhorred carbon for some obscure reason. The fate of our community of Greenies was different.

This is where the Templars enter the story. There are many tales about the Templars. There were also whispers that some at least were heretics. Well, green eyed envy ever besmirches the successful as well as the useful, and there's no doubt that the Templars were both successful and useful. Many were evidently pious and humble, even mystical, qualities often denigrated by the worldly.

It seems that the Templar Preceptor for this district took an interest in the fate of our local Greenies for some reason. Perhaps he may have liked their leader, who seems to have been a colorful character, noted in the stories under various pseudonyms such as "Arch-priest Jeremiah." In any case, as the local story goes, one afternoon the Preceptor paid a visit to the Arch-priest. The arrival of a group of well-armed and well mounted men in Templar uniform caused much perturbation in those who saw them pass, and who answered their polite request for directions to the dwelling of the Arch-priest, who lived in a big farmhouse with a group of his followers. The Petrine mutterings of these followers were quickly quelled by more thoughtful assessment of the Preceptor's escort of hard-faced war veterans. When it became clear that the Preceptor was there to visit the Arch-priest, but not to arrest him, the followers, although not the escort, relaxed.

The two men got on well. Both were well educated and well informed with broad interests. After the usual social preliminaries, such as discussion of the weather and the crop prospects, talk turned to religion, particularly the early history of Christianity. Was it chance or Providence that had decided which of the numerous schools of opinion were to flourish and be accepted as Orthodox, and which would be condemned as heretical? How strange it was that views at one time completely acceptable and spread by missionaries were later deemed unacceptable. What immense trouble the Christological disputes of Byzantine theologians had caused their state. How one of the Fathers of the Church had been condemned and excommunicated—two centuries after his death. How one of these holy men had written that whatever fables he had to tell the people, privately he would remain a philosopher. How St. Paul had said that he would be all things to all men to bring them to Christ. How some of the martyrs had been so in love with death that they had forced their prosecution upon reluctant officials. How some of the missionaries had adopted the local culture to facilitate the spreading of their gospel. How Pope Gregory had sent Augustine to England with instructions to take over pagan holy places and festivals and adapt them to Christianity. How the Bible famously allowed that "In my Father's house are many mansions," without defining them more closely. The Preceptor mentioned that although the attention of the Inquisition had been drawn to this area, they and his own organization were very busy. He and his superiors were hopeful that the Holy Spirit would soon lead an upsurge of faith in this district, whether through seeing the condign severity with which the pertinaciously contumacious were dispatched, or through the mercy with which God touched the hearts of sinners enabling their repentance, remained to be seen; although he personally prayed for the latter. The agents of the Inquisition were expected to arrive in no more than two weeks' time, then the answer might be revealed. The message having been obliquely but clearly delivered, the two men turned their attention to sampling and appraising the Arch-priest's supply of locally brewed beer. Pronouncing it good, the Preceptor and his men departed, leaving a thoughtful Arch-priest surrounded by inquisitive followers.

Next Sunday the Church of the Green Jesus opened for worship. When the Inquisition opened their inquiries in the district a week later, it sheltered many who might not have passed rigorous inspection otherwise. It was controversial from the start. Few believed in the sincerity of this sudden Damascene conversion, although all accepted that a visit from a Templar Preceptor just ahead of the arrival of the Inquisition could have induced a profound change of consciousness comparable to such an event. Seeing the light was obviously preferable to seeing the flames. Those few who felt otherwise had left to meet their fiery destiny elsewhere. Some of the Righteous were outraged; the self-righteous often are. Complaints to officialdom were met by references to motes and beams, the parable wherein the late recruited laborers received as much pay as those who had worked throughout the whole day, the return of the Prodigal Son, rejoicing over the salvation of lost lambs, injunctions to Christian charity, and much blandness. Naturally the members of this new church were closely observed, but no one found sufficient evidence against them to justify treating them as relapsed heretics, so the barking diminished as the caravan moved on.

For most of the Greenies it was a surprisingly easy change, once they were careful to adjust their rhetoric and nomenclature. "Global Warming" easily translated as "Hell." Strenuous personal efforts to avoid it, and widespread preaching to that effect, were standard and expected Christian practices. Satan and his minions easily substituted for big corporations. "Sin" replaced carbon in their diatribes. "Salvation" became of much greater relevance than technology. Personal austerity and not-too-pointed references to greed, corruption and hypocrisy were likewise accepted as normal. "Waste not, want not" and "You can't have your cake and eat it" were old saws. Proficiency in natural gardening and skill in handicrafts were useful and now necessarily becoming commonplace. Oil, or indeed "gas" in any form, and its products were no longer available to the general public, so tirades against them ceased as they became irrelevant. The historically inclined could discuss the history of Indulgences and of carbon trading. As usual, beards remained fashionable for reputed holy men, and now also for many others. Wild eyes and long robes remained optional. The translation and transition from a secular materialist frame of reference to a Christian religious one was not so difficult. As they ceased to stick out so egregiously, fewer of their neighbors felt that they were nails which needed to be hammered down. Indeed, as the Templar probably expected, after a couple of generations the members of the church would have been horrified had they been able to know and understand the true beliefs of their founders.

They quickly developed a distinctive brand, market niche or theological emphasis. A special devotion to St. Francis was part of it. Preaching to birds and beasts still seemed "far out," but the notion if not the practice, provided an acceptably Christian frame of reference for a religiously oriented concern with nature. The previous sentimentality about lambs had diminished as hunger and poverty made them again a profitable food source not often available to much of the population, rather than infantile woolly images of cloying sweetness. The Agnus Dei remained a highly acceptable religious symbol. Woolen textiles silently replaced synthetic materials that were no longer available. Shepherds were authentically Biblical characters and had a renewed economic significance. Speculation about the relation between their woolen clothing, the web of nature and the Seamless Robe of Christ which was divided by his persecutors, although it may have had the potential for heresy, was within acceptable bounds. Eucharistic symbolism easily extended from bread and wine to embrace mutton or lamb as the body of Christ, for those who could afford it, although officially only the former were Biblically endorsed for use in Holy Communion.

The pious legend of St. Hubert who beheld a crucifix between the horns of a stag provided inspiration for a local style of flowing art depicting not only the very

Biblical vines, figs and olive trees, but also deer nibbling the leaves of the Tree of Life, Noah's Ark, Elijah's ravens, lions and lambs, fishes, the Evangelical emblems of lion, man, eagle and bull, and any other reference to flora and fauna that could attest a more or less authentically Biblical provenance. No one caviled at the occasional mushroom in discreet corners of designs. Corn (all edible grain, not specifically maize) and wine were acceptable, and no one took it amiss if a special devotion to St. John Barleycorn was sometimes exuberantly expressed. Indeed, and not for the first time, other and sometimes older faiths were subsumed under the rubric of Christianity without much difficulty.

The state of innocence in this Edenic garden persisted for some years, or even decades. Eventually a smart young man named Jonas Caraway became prominent in this loose knit community. A throwback to an earlier era, he was definitely what had been known as a "go-getter." Jonas became a leader determined to craft an organization and a business model which would have substantial impact and outreach beyond the locality and its community or congregation. He forged the Church of the Green Jesus into a vehicle to serve his special devotion to money and self-publicity. His business talent soon created, if not an empire, then certainly a prosperous province in the world of recreational drug growing and distribution. The Church had become locally and discreetly known as a supplier of marijuana and "entheogenic" mushrooms, but Jonas turned it into a business, and combined the notions of business and cult. His early profits were ploughed back into the business, sprinkled liberally with pious references to the Parable of the Talents, and brought forth strange fruits. The acreage under cultivation was increased, the staff or congregation was "upgraded" and motivated to increase productivity, branch offices or Churches were opened across more and more of the country. "Bishop Jonas," as he rapidly became, and his supervisors or Canons, were soon known to be heavy handed and easily offended, but there was little adverse publicity, and "My God, how the money rolls in, rolls in!" was the overriding theme.

So far, so good. Or, so bad. A matter for the perhaps negligent or somnolent or corrupt local authorities and their perhaps incompetent or over-stretched police forces, but not something to gain widespread notoriety, you might think. So far you would be right. Jonas however had another gift, not exactly Eucharistic, a flair for self-publicity unfortunately combined with a sneering sense of his own cleverness. Not satisfied with success, Jonas had to improve upon it.

The original Church had a sign outside it, a literally green painted image of Jesus. Certainly distinctive, but not offensive. It is said that at first this image had been outlined by a sort of flashing green light which glowed in the dark, much used by the people in olden times. Believe that story if you will. In any case, as success went to his head, "Bishop" Jonas demonstrated his wit by revising the liturgy of his church, and then advertising it. Smoking a marijuana cigarette became the new sacrament, and he would place a burning "joint" in the mouth of the green image of Jesus, often standing outside the church building, laughing with passers-by and alternating the cigarette between his lips and those of Jesus, whilst garbed in his self-designed ecclesiastical cope which featured a huge green marijuana leaf on a golden background. Certainly distinctive, and very offensive. So far, so local.

A lamb not being enough, Jonas went for the sheep. As his cult expanded, he became more concerned with branding and advertising his products and himself. He packaged his products in green paper bearing a depiction of Jesus and himself standing together wearing Biblical robes and smoking marijuana cigarettes with the letters "J" and "C" over their respective heads and leering smiles on their faces. This Unique Selling Point certainly began to draw attention to him. His end was now inevitable, but just what the event was which lit the faggots he had so carefully placed around his own feet, remains obscure. One version is that a well-known minister of a more orthodox denomination pulled out a handkerchief at a church gathering and one of these lurid covers fluttered out of his pocket with it, to the scandal of the assembled dignitaries once one of them had retrieved it. Others suggest that business rivals who had their own discreet contacts, began to whisper more and more urgently into official ears as Jonas became more successful and as more evidence against him could be presented to the public. Out of sight, wheels began to turn, joints and bones began to crack, names began to be screamed, and the Hounds of God ran silently upon his trail.

They say he did not die well. He was not the only one to die of course. Most of his followers were caught, although a few probably escaped, and many of his customers and business contacts shared their fate. That's what made the name famous, or infamous, of course. Jonas wasn't the only person with a sense of drama and the ability to ensure that a message was heard loudly and clearly. His screams and babbling certainly were heard for hours. The executions were spread over the country and widely publicised. Special attention was devoted to the execution of "Bishop" Jonas. All local officials and prominent persons were required to attend. National dignitaries attended. The local populace, including the children, were also mostly assembled there, few exemptions were permitted. Deterrence is more effective if you see the pain, hear the screams and howls, smell the smoke and the roasting flesh, watch it basted in its own blood, track the melting and bubbling fat, smell the appetizing smell of roasting meat, see someone you once knew become an unrecognizable distorted blackened lump, still screaming, whilst his blood and sizzling fat and soot and ashes smears your own face. It helps if you puke your own guts out over your own and your neighbor's shoes, and hear their moans and sobs as well as your own all overlain by the howling of the object that had been a man. People remember that, and pass on the story to their grandchildren. The officials and dignitaries, although many blanched and gulped, did not lose their dignity by moaning or puking or turning their gazes away like women or children. No mercy was shown. The event lasted all morning. When it seemed he might die too soon, the fire was slaked, or raked back. Others who had not been adjudged so guilty had been allowed bags of gunpowder around their necks to end their misery much sooner, but this was denied to Jonas. He was no martyr. He had no cause but his own vanity. He lacked the dignity to die without whining and pleading and cursing uselessly. He deserved what happened to him. Some of the more hardened and stony-faced officials were able to sit smoking marijuana cigarettes as they watched. Another brand obviously. Marijuana is not illegal. Blasphemy is.

The little church fell upon hard times after that. It was abandoned for years and neglected as nobody was left to look after it and no group wished to be associated with its name, for fear of being regarded as surviving followers of Jonas. The name and the memory survived locally, of course, and people knew the stories associated with the little building and its strange image of Jesus. After various tramps and misfits who had drifted by and squatted in and around the building had become nuisances and been moved on feeling sore, another group crystallized there. They were known as Diggers, perhaps partly in reference to the seventeenth century sect and partly because they cultivated and searched for mushrooms and spent a lot of time grubbing around. Something of the ideas and stories surrounding the place filtered through to them and in local thought they assumed or resumed the group identity of the Church. This group however had somewhat different interests. This time it was mushrooms and symbiotic forms of life. Many of the stories associated with these people are extremely strange and disturbing. Some may be derived from what they themselves said. Others may have come from what was later gleaned by the inquiries of the Inquisition. It is widely accepted that mushrooms are the fruit of fungi which attach themselves to the roots of trees. They said that the trees and the fungi exchanged food, much like, they also said, people and plants exchange different types of air. Maybe they did know more than ordinary people; I can't say.

The stories began to get a bit scary when they said such things as that trees could make their leaves poisonous to dissuade or kill animals which over-grazed them, and warn each other when the animals started to munch on one of them, and transfer food or water to each other via their roots and networks of fungi. There were creepy echoes of ancient stories of people being lost in a forest where the trees slowly closed in on them, or of Triffids and Venus fly traps. From the olden days came a legend that the great trees of the Pacific Northwest coast had been fed on salmon by the bears which guarded them. There were whispers of bugs which got into mice, and caused them to act counter to their natural instincts and to seek out cats rather than flee from them, and hints that something similar could hap-

pen to people, maybe spread by parasitic fungi. Perhaps there was a natural muta-
tion or some form of ghoulish experiment went wrong—or right. Concern definitely became Inquisitorial when rumors spread that they worshiped and had
communion with the spirits of trees and desert cacti and vines from distant forests;
but that must have come a lot later. Obviously the only Biblical spin on anything
which smacked of Sacred Groves or High Places or relations with unclean spirits led
straight through the fire to Hell. At the time of course, their neighbors would not
have seen anything very strange about these people. Tending to one's trees and to
one's garden and to one's own business was absolutely normal. Only later could
people wonder whether these folk had somehow become taken over by their trees,
mentally controlled by them and used as ambulant servitors. That after all would
not have been so different from how plants used animals and insects to spread their
pollen and their seeds. Maybe, as with fungi, they became more tightly and physically linked. Very nice for the trees if they could get people to bring them food
and water, spread and plant their seeds and generally act as their gardeners. Fungi,
trees, humans, each making use of the others. Was any one of them in charge? If
plants could create scents and colors to attract insects, and some could give humans
intense emotional and mystical experiences, perhaps they would provide some kind
of feelings of happiness or even bliss to keep their human labor force content and
productive. It's only a couple of steps further to have them lay down their lives and
those of others for their owners.

A new artistic motif began to be noticed in association with the Church of the
Green Jesus and its followers and hangers-on. That was the Green Man, a revival of
a much older image, a man's head peeking through foliage. No satisfactory explanation was ever offered, although later there was speculation as to whether it
might have meant something. A wild natural consciousness perhaps, or human intelligence expressed through vegetable life, or a man assimilated to a tree maybe. If
the Inquisition couldn't settle the question, neither can I.

What was later settled was that The Men of the Green Lord as some of them
called themselves (O shades of Osiris!) had formed a cult somewhat along the lines
of the Thugs. They became great travelers, working as artists, carvers, tinkers, con-
jurors, entertainers, gardeners and plant distributors and so forth. They spread the
image along with the cult, and used it as a recognition sign, rather as the early
Christians had used the fish. They did not use the name of the Church of the
Green Jesus, nor create local "branches"—hmm. At first they tended to return
there each year as a kind of general meeting place, and some of their gains, well or
ill-gotten, were used to maintain it and its surroundings. It was probably rather
beautiful, and their influence created a modest prosperity in several local businesses. They even established their own passenger and freight haulage businesses.
"Tree Line" or "Green Way" or something twee like that I think they may have

been called. They are said to have acquired property in the district and to have created gardens open to the public, and their devotion to composting and mulching became well known.

All good things come to an end, they say. I suppose the same may be said of bad or indifferent things, although they are less wistfully missed. In this case, the end began far away in a town where the Green Men had established several of their organizations. There are always a certain number of missing people. Sometimes they are found, in good or in bad condition. Sometimes they do not want to be found. Sometimes there is a hue and cry, particularly if the missing person is either a person of consequence, or a child or someone else about whose imagined fate a great deal of popular sentiment may easily and profitably be stirred up.

"Ah, you just can't get the staff these days, can you?" Excessively rapid expansion of an organization, unrestrained ambition, lack of supervision and training, low quality of staff, lack of due diligence and risk assessment, all these and other familiar terms of business "cant" may have played a part in their downfall. Along with bad luck, fate, the wrath of God, or probability, perhaps.

It was of course a huge scandal. Several entangled scandals, in fact. As the rigorous investigations of the judicial and Inquisitorial authorities established (and we may be fully confident that there was nothing slipshod in *their* work), a couple of low level Green Men had decided to improve their prospects by developing an unofficial line in kidnapping. Their victim, the son of a successful businessman (and indeed, why would anyone kidnap the son of an unsuccessful one?), had escaped from the inadequately secured shed in which they had left him inadequately secured whilst they went on an alcoholic spree to discuss their future plans, none of which were to come to fruition in their actual future, short as it was to be. This shed was located in the "staff only" yard at the back of one of the public gardens which they maintained. When the police arrived, in force need we say, their curiosity extended to the rest of the area. One of its facilities was a small bone crushing plant which produced the bone meal used for horticultural purposes. Some of the as yet uncrushed bones aroused suspicion, which forensic examination of the bones and of the meal justified, by confirming that they were human remains. Remains of whom, and where were the remaining remains, so to speak?

The opportunity to close many missing person cases stimulated police investigation in other districts, once news spread, and as the reluctance of detained persons associated with Green Men organizations to assist these inquiries was overcome, it spread fast. All the faster because of another interrelated scandal. In the course of investigating the gardening businesses in adjacent districts for more human bones, the murdered and abused corpse of a missing infant was discovered in a compost heap of one of their businesses. This child had been missing for some weeks and already there had been considerable public agitation about her fate. That nailed them. (NO! NO! Not literally! That would have been blasphemous. We certainly don't want to give a wrong impression about anything which the Inquisition might find objectionable. Do you?) I mean, there was so much public outcry that investigation focused on them even more intensely. Although it was the corpse of that sadly mistreated infant which made them monsters in the public mind, the Green Men steadfastly denied any involvement in or knowledge about her death. Some went to their deaths denying it after they had admitted other killings, and protesting that it would not have been a good way to prepare compost. It may be that it was just a coincidence and some other murderer escaped justice when they were blamed.

The investigators found that not only did the Green Men murder people for no better motive than to use their bodies to nourish trees and other plants, they had done so for many years, and made a profit from their sales of plant food. This news make many people look a bit askance at their crops and gardens, wondering just whose remains might be helping them to thrive, and resulting in a drop in the popularity of such products. A bit strange really, as people have no objection to eating plants and know that their own bodies will go back to the soil, "dust to dust; ashes to ashes," potentially to nourish plants in their turn, but people are not altogether rational. It was soon seen that there was a strong correlation between the growth of Green Man activity in an area and reports of missing persons. Indeed, increases in such reports were able to indicate areas where they were operating without as yet establishing organizations associated with them. Initially investigators thought they were dealing with a criminal organization following a bizarre business model. It had few links to the recognized criminal underworld, however. It was puzzling that many of the corpses were not turned into profit, but chopped up and buried near trees, often in the gardens and parks which the Green Men maintained. Sometimes portions of the bodies had been transported long distances to be buried under special trees rather than disposed of more conveniently. Indeed, at first the authorities had not realized that the connections went beyond the particular businesses and that the Green Man image was actually associated with them and involved people who had no connection with these businesses, and that the image, when it came to their attention, was the key to understanding events. It was when the authorities discovered that such burials were not just a convenient way to conceal a murder, but were the motive for the murder—and furthermore, that it was the preferred method of the leading lights for their own interment, and that these leading lights had a special fondness or devotion for individual trees—that things became really serious. The hints of an organized religious cult underlying these strange and repulsive happenings, and their hysterical magnification by the popular press, immediately elevated the matter from the criminal, past the political, to the religious plane.

It was an immense embarrassment. The country had been infiltrated by a well organized, extensive and criminal organization, and much worse—an evil pagan cult—without the authorities having been aware of its existence and of the dangers it posed. They first found out about it by reading the popular press! How was this possible? Why had the Inquisition, the organization tasked with protecting the morals and religious purity of the population and the state, not detected and eliminated this danger? This last question was certainly raised in high places, although the press had the prudence not to do more than hint at it. *Quis custodiet ipsos custodes?* was a question in many minds, but sensibly it was never publicly asked.

With so much egg dripping from important and humorless faces, someone was going to fry. Or roast. Many did. How then did the little church survive? Perhaps it had some luck, but by then it was no longer central, or even of interest to the Green Men. Their operations had spread far afield, and the businesses which were to prove fatal had not been operated here. Any connection with local disappearances long ago was not queried. The discreet graves of the founders under their favorite trees, or their successors, were not remembered and not disturbed. Its name was not used so no connection was identified. It may be that there were a few convenient deaths or disappearances which broke any living links between the Green Men and the Green Jesus before the authorities reached them. Now the tangle of tales is only of interest to a few antiquarians such as ourselves, although the Church remains part of local lore and its green image, somewhat restored, may still be seen. The Green Man is no longer a popular artistic motif around here, but you may still find a few such heads near old graves under the trees. Sometimes it's even possible to imagine such likenesses in knotty branches or roots.

Yes, we can visit it. It's not far to walk, although there's not a great deal to see. I like to stroll or sit under the trees about the area, and help to keep the place tidy. It's very peaceful there, although sometimes strange thoughts come to me. What might happen, for instance, if we took the notion of a Green Jesus seriously? What if the Second Coming has already occurred, and we missed it? "When Jesus came to Birmingham they merely passed him by," a poet wrote. What if he was here and we didn't notice? What if he's still waiting for us? What if this time he came, not as a human, but as a tree? What if we considered the Holy Cross seriously? "He came to his own and his own received him not." Has the plant kingdom received him in our stead? Has he been there all along, but we have been too thick to notice? What about the Real Presence of divinity in bread and wine? What about the myth of the Tree of Life? After the Norse Ragnarok they expected a new humanity to emerge from the Tree to repopulate the earth. What about that? The early depictions of Jesus on the Cross showed him in majesty, with arms outstretched, outlined by but not bound to the "Tree" as it was often called. Only later was there a change to depictions of a literal crucifixion. Enough questions before we attract the attention of a literal Inquisition.

Here we are. That's the famous wooden image of the Green Jesus. I'll just wait and sit under the trees there while you look around. Sometimes it seems so beautiful that one's spirit is uplifted and one seems to share with nature in some great rite or hymn of praise. Hearing the leaves rustle one may fancy one almost hears what the Lord God said to Adam when they walked together in that Garden, or what Lord Zeus spoke through Dodona's oak. Perhaps if you are deemed worthy you may hear the answer. Ah yes, there it is. When the light is right it shimmers on the Green Jesus as if it was gold, and He may smile or even wink.

AN EXPECTED CHILL
BY JOEL CARIS

LINSEY WOKE HARD INTO DARKNESS. Lying on her back, she blinked up at the just visible ceiling, then shifted her attention to the soft outline of their bedroom window. Early. She guessed 5:30—earlier than she normally woke. Brett slept next to her, curled on his side and breathing easy and rhythmic, unperturbed by her sudden consciousness. Listening to him, she thought a moment about trying to return to sleep—join him in oblivion—but knew it was no use. The events from the day before already tugged at her, threatened to set her mind moving in directions she didn't need. So, pushing back the covers, she slipped out of bed and moved soft through the room, quiet but not too quiet. Brett slept deep most of the time. She rarely woke him.

An expected chill pervaded the apartment, and she grabbed a pair of thick wool socks from one of the open drawers of their dresser as she passed. She put them on in the bathroom, along with a heavy robe, and then shuffled into the kitchen for her morning ritual: a small cup of coffee, not too weak but not strong, made from a small scoop of their precious grounds; a piece of bacon fried in a cast iron skillet, followed by two eggs and pan-fried toast; a small glass of goat milk. She had her routine down perfect. She finished the pour over coffee just as she pulled the eggs and toast from the skillet, sliding them onto her plate, taking it all to their small dining table.

The clock only just ticking over to six, she sat relishing her first sips of coffee and then cut into her eggs while reflecting on her early awakening. She would have liked it to be the cold morning or her anticipation for the day's harvest, but knew neither of those things had awoken her. No, it came from the death and unrest the day before, and from the sickening anticipation of what might be to come. The city had started to break yesterday, frustrations pouring into the streets. She worried that flood would continue and start tearing apart her community and the modest life Brett and she had made over the past few years. She wanted to help piece it all back together, but knew she had no domain over the situation. It would run its course regardless.

Her small comfort that morning lay in thoughts of her winter squash crop and the wealth it represented. With the chill from the night before, the frost out on the grass, she felt certain it would be waiting for her this morning, touched finally by sweetness and ready for harvest. She didn't know what else might be waiting, though, and that worried her.

A half hour later, breakfast eaten and dishes washed, she knelt by the bed and snaked her arms around Brett, still sleeping, breaths still so heavy. He stirred as she kissed him on the cheek, then at the corner of his eye, and he smiled as he opened to the sight of her. "Hi," he said, sleepy.

"Hi," she said back.

"It's early."

"Yeah. Sorry, I wanted to say goodbye."

"Don't be sorry," he said. He put a hand on her back, pressing light. "Squash today?"

"I think so. I'll see how it feels, but it's cold out there." She hesitated. "You?"

"I'm gonna clear that bed for the garlic." Now *he* hesitated. "Jack said he may need help with the solar heater, the plumbing for it. I'll check in with him. It'd be good to learn." This dance of theirs—it made her sick, worry on top of apprehension, the layers suffocating her. "You have Katherine today?" he asked.

"She'll be there," Linsey said, adjusting herself back to see him better, bring his guarded face into better focus.

"Okay. I can come by and help get the squash in if you want."

He glanced down a moment, away from her—somewhere else. "We can get it done," she said. "Katherine's fast—she's a damn workhorse." She paused. "You should learn plumbing."

He stared at her a moment—blinking slow, then touching the back of her neck, resting his hand there—and she thought of their conversation last night, of the people flooding into the streets. It amped him, she knew, made him want to burn. Made him want the struggle, which scared the hell out of her. "What do you think's going to happen today?" he asked.

She sighed. "I don't know, babe. I don't know if I want to know. I just want to harvest and feel rich."

He smiled at that. "Me too."

"You want that?"

"I want it for you."

His hand felt hot on her neck. "You don't want it for us?" she asked. "You want something else?"

He shook his head, and the silence stretched a moment while he stared lost at her. "I don't believe you," she said. "You always want something else."

Pulling his hand away, taking a deep breath—she knew too well the ways he fell into himself, all the fights he fought in his head without her. He looked at the ceiling for a moment, then back at her. "I just want the world okay for us," he said. "I . . . just want to do what's right."

"Yeah," she said, her voice rising. "Well, I think gardening and plumbing and bringing in the squash is what's right. It's what needs to be done—for us, for other people, for this stupid city that's trying to tear itself apart. That's what we have to do, you know. We don't get to throw our lives aside every time people get crazy. And we don't have to tear ourselves apart just because they are."

"I know," he lied, looking away from her.

Silence again while she struggled to know what to say—how to close their divide before she left. But there was no reason she would know it any better now than she had in the past—hell, even the night before. She stood, bent down and kissed him quick. "Eat a good breakfast. Work. And just . . . ignore the bullshit outside, okay? I'm not saying forever, but . . . I can't, okay? I just want you here for dinner. I want you to tell me about plumbing, and I want to tell you about squash, and I want us to have this place, okay? Have each other." She hated her voice then, but knew nothing else to do.

"I know," he said, watching her with so much he wouldn't say. "Okay."

"Fuck." She stared at him. "I love you, and I wish you would—"

—*not be stupid.*

"I know," he said, sliding his hand over her calf, his tone an apology.

So often able to read her mind.

Normally she would bike to the Sixth, but that morning she walked. She wanted the cold air and its clarity, to see where the frost was and wasn't. She also wanted to listen and look and see if anything was yet happening in the city, or if the tension was still building behind closed doors and out of sight. Maybe more than all that, she wanted the rhythm of the walk and the way it allowed her to think, though her parting conversation left her doubtful of the utility of such time. Helpful thinking too often turned to harmful dwelling and she was already too at risk of that.

Pulling her heavy work coat tight around her, she walked at a brisk pace, eager for the warmth it would bring. The neighborhood spread quiet around her, the sky above still dark and only just starting to lighten, the stars beginning their fade into daylight banishment. Thanks to the city's budget cuts, only the occasional street light burned. She walked in shadow and dark far more often than not. It made her somewhat nervous, but she still liked it—some small reminiscence of her times lived in rural areas. Plus, she wanted this small stretch of dark before twilight broke it into a new day. She wanted this moment of quiet and calm.

Many of the houses were dark with slumber as she passed them. But a number of windows were lit, too, and she wondered in particular about the covered ones, about what was happening within. Were they making plans, plotting their anger? Or just getting ready for work as she had been shortly ago? Maybe eating breakfast and nothing more.

Doesn't matter anyway, she thought. *I've got my own crops to tend.*

The sun broke across the sky as she arrived at the Sixth, its orange glow heavy behind the tree line, altering the world's colors. She approached her plot from the south, along a small gravel road—or more a path, really, not that much wider than the golf carts that used to run it. Her work spread out in front of her, an overgrown and in many places ragged tangle of a vegetable plot, nearly an acre, spread with a wide array of vegetables and herbs, perennials, bordered by young fruit trees, many of the plants already harvested and left broken apart on the ground, but a good number of fall and winter crops yet to provide meals across the city. She winced a little at the mess of it, admonishing herself for not being tidier, not having it as clean and presentable as, say, the Council might like. But then, the purpose of it was to feed people and make a living, not to beautify the city under the shallowest of definitions. The sheer amount of good food resting here was beauty enough.

She allowed an initial survey of the plants—a small, ritual refamiliarizing that settled her without fail—before making the trek to the Clubhouse to pick up supplies, check in and make her presence official. Garrett waited there as always, nodded, dutifully logged her and her supplies: clippers, gloves, two hori-horis, a couple hand hoes. They chatted for a few moments—skirting around the clashes from the day before, too aware of the complex conflicts of interest littered across the former golf course. The subject felt too fraught for such an early morning interaction; might as well play safe. She did ask him, though, if there had been any trouble the night before—a concern of hers.

"Nope," he said, voice slow as always. "Or if so, they did it quiet and low key. No one's complained yet."

"How many are here?"

He smiled. "Just you."

"Really? Not even Nikki?"

"Haven't seen her."

"You take a walk this morning?"

"Of course," he said, shooting her a look. "I always do."

"Sorry, I know. I just mean—it look okay?"

"Yep, sure does. I guess I'll hear about it if it's not, though."

"I'm sure you will," Linsey said, then gave him her goodbye as she headed back for her plot, carrying her basket of supplies, suddenly wanting to take a closer look just to be sure. In the first few years Links had been active, no one had yet to engage in any significant vandalism of any of the plots, despite the acrimony over the decision to transition the golf course. The early going had been bumpy but successful, the controversy giving way to glowing media accounts and a thriving, twice-weekly on-site market. Garrett, a wealth of cameras, and a part time security guard turned out to be enough to patrol and keep stable the relatively open stretch of land within the city. Occasional thefts happened and kids sometimes acted their age—stomped a pumpkin, tagged a neighbor's door with stolen tomatoes—but there seemed a surprising level of respect and pride for the farm throughout the city. Of course, the stiff penalties for damaging city property didn't hurt and these days, as well, not many people looked askance at a solid source of food within city limits.

Still, the unrest the day before had been the worst to roil the city since Links had been christened, and respect for city property hadn't been particularly high the day before. She would hope that wouldn't extend to urban farmers and the land they leased, but who was to say? Some thought they were too tied to the Council, too buddy-buddy with the people in ever-more-tentative power. She would have enjoyed a long, clarifying conversation with such people, though they would be even more distrustful of her than any of the other Links farmers.

On return to her plot and a slow walk through it—needed, anyway, so she could categorize and prioritize tasks—she found her worries unfounded. The crops appeared as healthy as the day before, aside from those the light frost had left bowed and blackened. The basil was officially finished, tomatoes gone, her already-faded summer crops finished off for good. She expected it, of course, and it was really the squash she gave the closest look to. And indeed, as hoped for, it appeared ready for harvest, with the slightest of small discolorations on the skin, the flesh inside undoubtedly sweetened by the touch of frost. It would be a good harvest. Now she just had to pull in the few thousand pounds of fruit that awaited her. She would need to check out a cart and trailer from Garrett.

Pulling her pocket watch, she saw that she had a good hour before Katherine would arrive. Taking a pair of clippers from the supply basket, she got to work, pushing aside her worries and wondering what the brightening day would bring: hoping for simple harvest but suspecting worse.

‡‡

It didn't take long for Linsey to fall into the rhythm of the work, stepping carefully through the tangled squash vines, hunting down their fruit—sometimes visible, sometimes hidden in the tumble of foliage—and cutting their thick stems from the vines. She pushed the plants away from the fruit after each cut, making sure she could see it for its later move out of the field. Taking her time, enjoying the meditation of it, she worked steady through the crop. The variety of the harvest cheered her: Butternut, Delicata, Spaghetti, Carnivale, Sweet Meat, Kabocha, Acorn, and so many more, including experimental varieties. She always struggled to settle on a reasonable number of varieties deep in the winter, when she found herself sorting through the special order seed catalogs from the small companies proliferating throughout the Northwest.

The public's increasing, almost pathological demand for variety and heirloom revivals didn't help her. As home gardens and small farms continued to boom, and more municipalities pursued urban farming policies to secure local food supplies, small seed companies focused on regional varieties and those tailored to a wide array of micro-climates began multiplying at a dizzying rate, spread by the technological failures and devastating public backlash against the corporate seed companies. Linsey had found it a blessing and a curse. On one hand, too many new ventures kept coming to market with weak seed that sometimes didn't breed true, their owners hampered by lack of experience and knowledge. Yet a number of new breeders were pushing deep into genetic localization and increased resiliency to the wild swings in weather becoming more common as the global climate continued to spiral deeper into chaos and unpredictability. As a farmer and someone who, at a basic level, simply loved plants, she found the diversity exciting and always looked forward to long winter afternoons spent combing through seed catalogs and participating in the ritual discovery of new varieties. However, the small nagging always remained in the back of her head: this breakneck search for the next great seed was as much frantic safeguarding against the knife's edge of too little to eat. Too many massive crop failures had unfolded over the proceeding years. Too many food riots haunted countries across the globe, including America. The last few years, she had been waiting for the next shoe to drop.

Of course, she had learned long ago that ignoring the tasks at hand while waiting for the next dark turn in America's stumble down the world pecking order was a fool's game. Too much good work needed to be done and, as she walked through the squash now—clipping and turning, admiring the fruit—the satisfaction of that work settled deep into her, providing some of the limited control over her life she still felt she had these days. Pride settled in, as well—her usual reaction to a good harvest. There was little more satisfying than seeing such an impressive spread of food and sustenance she knew came in large part from her own labor and skill. It made her feel powerful.

Katherine arrived as Linsey moved through the final row of squash, her rusted bike bouncing hard and fast along the pathway, coming in from the south the same as Linsey had earlier. She came to a quick stop, gravel scattering from beneath the bike's tires. "Hey," she said, breath heavy as she dismounted the bicycle and let it drop to the ground, then shrugged off her backpack and dropped it, too. Her first day on the job, Linsey had made clear to Katherine she was not to treat any of her tools or other equipment in a similar fashion, or she would risk her wrath and a quick bounce from the Sixth. Katherine told her not to worry, no problem, and she stayed true to that assurance from the first day. Numerous times Linsey had seen Katherine abuse her own belongings, but she always treated others' with the utmost care. It made little sense to Linsey—her disregard for her own belongings—but sometimes that was all the sense she could hope to make of Katherine. She loved her to death just the same.

As Linsey quickly clipped her way down the final row, Katherine swapped out her top shirt with her usual farm flannel, ragged and familiar, permanently stained with dirt and plant matter. "So it's ready," Katherine said, looking over the sea of squash vines, many of them now ragged and broken thanks to Linsey's efforts.

"It's ready," Linsey said, clipping a final squash and straightening up at the end of the row, turning to appraise her work. "At least, I hope. I've got it all clipped."

Turning back, she saw Katherine stretching and smiling, but with dark eyes that belied her expression. "So now we haul."

"Now we haul," Linsey agreed. "Let's line them up by variety along the edge here," she said, motioning down at the three foot strip of grass between the squash beds and the gravel path. "Then we can go get the cart from Garrett and start getting them to storage."

Katherine clapped, short and sharp, her usual enthusiastic start to work. But it felt different today to Linsey, empty, a show of expected behavior rather than genuine enthusiasm.

"Let's go," Katherine said.

They went.

Back and forth they walked, up and down the rows, filling their arms with squash large and small and bringing them to a gentle deposit on the grass by the side of the field. They worked quietly at first and nothing was odd about that. Katherine always worked quietly at first after an initial burst of enthusiasm upon arrival, moving fast and steady as though she wanted to accomplish a good chunk of the task at hand before daring to break the silence with conversation. Linsey never had figured out if it was a matter of ethic, a desire to come across as a good and hard worker, or just a natural internal rhythm of hers that demanded a bout of hard work before words could flow. It was her usual approach, though, so the silence didn't feel out of the ordinary at first.

Linsey couldn't help but watch her, though, as she gathered and moved the squash, stepping fast and graceful through the vines, showing an impressive ability to balance multiple large and misshapen fruit in her arms as she moved. Despite her fast work, something felt off with her—an unnecessary rigidity and intensity of focus. Normally, her quiet would not extend to lack of acknowledgment; she would still make the occasional non-leading comment or smile at inadvertent eye contact. But today she worked inside herself, it seemed, eyes often on the ground and not even the most passing of comment uttered.

She wondered if the city's angry energy was getting to Katherine, too, the same as it had cut her own sleep short that morning. She hoped not; Katherine's enthusiasm consistently heartened and helped carry her on days she struggled and she hated the thought of her being brought down by the stupidity and destructive lashings out around them.

Shrugging it off—Katherine would talk if she wanted to—she let her mind wander elsewhere as she moved the squash, back and forth, the rhythm of the work again settling into her. It didn't wander far, though, before finding the familiar rut of the day before, tracing the outpouring of anger and frustration across the city and her own foreboding sense that the life she had so carefully cultivated over the past two years might be dangling above some unexpected cliff, at the mercy of—

"Jesse was there yesterday," Katherine said.

Bent over and about to pick up a large Sweet Meat squash, Linsey looked up at Katherine, standing a few feet away and holding a Delicata squash and staring at her intense, all of her struggling. She looked close to tears; she looked ready to throw the squash; she looked ready to drill herself down into the earth and not emerge for a very long time. For a moment, Linsey felt dumb, her mind working over the words and trying to make sense of them.

Then she understood. "Up north. You mean at the shooting?"

"The fucking *murder*," she said, her voice straining, head nodding.

"He was there?"

"At the edge, part of the protest. Just—"

"Is he okay?"

She shook her head. "I guess, I don't know. He got knocked down, kicked, his shoulder . . . he said after the shots, it was everyone running and chaos. He was on the ground, everyone around him—he couldn't get up. That's when his shoulder got hurt. Somebody kicked him hard, probably just on accident."

"But he's okay?"

"He—" she shrugged, gestured, and the Delicata slipped out of her hands, hit the ground below. Katherine looked down at it, lying in the dirt, then up at Linsey.

"I'm sorry."

"Shit," Linsey said. She stepped through the squash, broad leaves hooking and giving against her feet, the vines snapping with only the smallest resistance. "Come here." She motioned over toward the already-moved squash, the stretch of clear grass. "Come on." Katherine moved, her head down, still stepping so damn careful. *It doesn't fucking matter*, Linsey wanted to say, the squash already done, not important anyway. But she was so careful with the things that weren't hers. She could never bear to hurt what wasn't hers to hurt.

She grabbed Katherine, held her tight. The girl—then, anyway; a girl then—slipped her arms around her but didn't cry. Still held. "Is he home?" Linsey asked.

"Yeah," she said, voice still tight, her chin on Linsey's right shoulder. "The police sent him to the hospital for his shoulder but then held him, questioned him. He said they seemed suspicious, but he didn't . . . he was just there, that's all."

"How close?"

"I don't know."

"Did he see?"

"I don't know."

"Did he—"

"*Linsey*." She pulled back, looked at her. "I *don't know*."

Linsey put a hand against the side of her head. "I'm sorry," she said, looking past Katherine at the trees beyond, the lightened autumn sky. Turning leaves and green of pine needles. The traced outline of the natural world, always continuing on while the rest of them fought and tumbled in the background. "I'm sorry."

Word of the shooting came in confused flashes. No, first it came in the sirens screaming everywhere. Linsey had been working the Sixth the day before, Katherine taking her usual Wednesday off. She had been in the squash then, too, walking and inspecting it and thinking, with the expected chill that night, that it would finally be ready for harvest the next day. It took her a moment to recognize the sirens, to actually hear them, and then they seemed all around her. Off somewhere else but coming from every direction. A lot of them, at least two different pitches. Police and ambulance for sure.

She didn't usually hear so many, but otherwise she let it be. Sirens came and went in the city and besides, she had work to do. They didn't get too close, and that was good enough for her. No one at Links was injured. Nothing untoward had happened on one of the other holes. She kept inspecting the squash, then began turning a bed in anticipation of planting garlic, the seed in for both the Sixth and their home garden. It was one of her favorite tasks, flipping the beds and turning the soil with her digging fork. She lost herself in it.

It wasn't until checking in with Garrett at the end of the day that he told her about the rumors flying, the online reports still as yet unverified. A shooting had taken place in the northern section of the city, at least two people dead. Supposedly it was private security hired by Helton that had committed the murders, a forced eviction of squatters that had spiraled out of control. Supposedly protesters had shown up, a crowd gathering and quickly erupting into shouts and intimidation, a surge against the hired guns. Supposedly they shot indiscriminately; supposedly they were only protecting themselves. The police had arrived to a scene of madness. No one gave them advance notice of the eviction. No one really knew anything, except that the city was beginning to devolve into chaos and protests were breaking out in every quadrant, questionable reports of rioting spreading throughout the city.

Linsey biked home fast at that point, eager to check in with Brett, her eyes sharp for riots. She saw none, but heard chatter and watched other bikers pass her fast, looking intent. Maybe it meant nothing, maybe everything. When she arrived home, he wasn't there and she called Jack. He knew nothing except that Brett had worked the morning and then left. Cursing his lack of a cell phone—on board normally with the decision and not owning one herself, but just wanting to talk with him—she waited. He straggled in hours later, exhausted and amped, his jittery edge telling her all she needed to know even before he spoke. He'd been marching and the police broke it up. He fumed at the murder and told her what he knew, which was little. She didn't even know if it *was* murder, though Helton's behavior had been skirting the edge for months now, them taking more of the law into their own hands with each passing week and every new house and apartment building they bought up, increasing their grip on the city.

"They were arresting people, but I kept ahead," he said.

She stared at him, thinking so many things. "I wish you had been here when I got home," she said.

He watched her. "I couldn't stay here, Linsey."

"You couldn't stay here for me?"

"I had to go out there. It wasn't about you."

"Yeah," she said. "I figured."

His face told her he didn't think she was being fair. She didn't know if she was or not, and the conversation deteriorated from there into frustration, into fear, until finally she just lay down and closed her eyes and gave up trying to put it all together in a way that made sense—him piecing together a meal in the kitchen and her waiting for him to come to her and for them to try again.

Linsey and Katherine sat close together on the grass at the edge of the field, more than a thousand pounds of squash haphazardly piled around them and down the stretch of the field's edge, separated out more or less by variety. Katherine leaned against her and they both stared out at the line of fir trees just past the gravel path, their branches tangled and dark green against the deep blue sky echoing behind them. The morning was getting ready to give way to afternoon and the sun against Linsey had started to warm her, radiating in through her coat, readying her to shed layers. She slipped her arms around Katherine's shoulders and hugged her tight.

As they hauled in more of the squash, Katherine had already given her more of the story: Jesse calling late at night from the hospital and wanting to speak to their father; Katherine grilling him about where he was and what had happened, growing more anxious as it became clear something bad had happened; her finally passing the phone to her father, Francis, and then listening to his side of the conversation, all clipped sentences and assurances coupled with guarded but anxious glances at Katherine, his face slouched with weariness.

Now Linsey and Katherine had stopped for a break and, sitting in the grass, Katherine continued her story. "He works so hard for us," she told Linsey of her father, staring intense at her a moment. It wasn't often she talked about her father, but it always came with clear affection when she did. Linsey had met him once, a slight and burdened man who nonetheless spoke with a spark in his voice and an openness to life that caught her by surprise. She had liked him off the bat. "It killed me seeing him that worried and tired, because I hate seeing him hurt like that. I know how hard he works, everything he does for us, and . . . I just want to take that from him. Or at least help him. So I wanted to go with him to the hospital, but he said no. And I—" she paused, breathed. "I argued—I *fucking argued*—and I told him I was going to the hospital with him, that there was no damn way I wasn't, and he finally just told me that he couldn't have me there while he was trying to help Jesse, that he couldn't be split between us both. And . . . I know what he meant. It pissed me off because I was going down there to *help*, to help Jesse *and* him, but I know he can't do it that way. He has to be the one to do it and he can't share it with me, he can't give me any of that responsibility." She stared off into the distance and shook her head. "He never does it for the important things."

Linsey paused, but Katherine said no more. "So they came home?" she prompted.

"Yeah. It was an hour at least and they were both so tired. Jesse's shoulder was bandaged up and I could tell it hurt. A lot. But he wouldn't complain and . . . he didn't tell me much. Just what I told you." She paused and took a deep breath that turned into a sigh. "They both just went to bed. They were so tired."

They both fell silent. Linsey thought of Brett out on the streets, pressed into thick crowds of protestors, feeding off their energy. She imagined them all clawing at the air, fighting their existence, pressing hard in against men with guns and screaming for some kind of legitimacy and justice. In some ways she understood and in other ways . . . she felt the squash piled high around her, the plants breathing at her and Katherine's backs, the sky spiraling behind the trees and, beyond that, a quiet pond dotted with birds, a stilled and elegant Blue Heron likely somewhere in there; she had seen them before. Sometimes she didn't know the right way to make her life—only the way to keep making the one she already had.

"What do you think is going to happen?" Katherine asked.

Linsey hesitated. "What do you mean?"

"Here in the city, I guess. There are so many angry people."

"I keep wondering that."

"It pisses me off," Katherine said, after a silence. "It pisses me off that Helton can buy up every goddamn house in the city and kick people out and take their homes from them. It pisses me off that they can murder people and the police don't do anything—the Council doesn't do anything. It pisses me off how hard my dad works and how he's always behind. It pisses me off that he's doing it for *me* and that I can't yet take that from him." Katherine clutching at her thigh, pressing her thumbs deep into the flesh as she stared out at the trees beyond. Linsey put her hand over Katherine's, breaking the grip, and the girl stared down at Linsey's hand over her own and shook her head. "It pisses me off that he went out there, that he was *there*, that he could have gotten himself killed. And it pisses me off that I wasn't there with him even though I wasn't working, even though I could have gone, could have tried to help him break their grip on the city, could have *done* something."

"Katherine—"

"*Somebody* has to do something, Linsey."

"I know, Katherine, but that's it? That's the something? You go out and fight and yell until another person's dead and everyone else wants to burn the city to the ground?"

Katherine stared at her for a moment and then flickered her eyes past her, beyond, focused somewhere distant. "It's already burning," she said, and her gaze flicked back to Linsey. "You want to ignore it?"

"No."

"Then what?"

"I just—" She turned, looking back at the beds spread behind her, so much food and work stretching toward the course's edge. She remembered the first weeks of the season, her and Katherine turning the soil by hand and shaping the beds, a season of potential accomplishment stretched out before them. Every year she just wanted to feed people. Every year it kept her going until the next, even as the world kept breaking around her. "I don't want to lose the difference I make."

Katherine gave her a sad smile, and then even that faded. "I don't know that it's yours to lose," she said. Again her eyes flicked past Linsey, off somewhere distant and likely unseen. As she spoke again, it came out soft and melancholy. "It may just be taken from you," she said, and then after a beat stood to start working again.

They eventually broke for lunch and then returned to work, the rest of the day passing with few words and a good deal of exertion. Checking out an old electric golf cart with a small trailer attachment from Garrett, they moved the squash harvest up to the Clubhouse and into cool storage—a closed, dark room kept at a steady fifty degrees and sealed off from rodents, one of the infrastructural bequeathments that came with a plot at Links. They sorted the squash by variety into various bins and Linsey labeled them well to ensure that no other farmer took a share of harvest that wasn't theirs. Between good labeling, the decency of the people who farmed at Links, the check-in desk, and the small, always-recording camera recessed into a corner of the storage room, everyone stayed honest.

By the time they had harvested, sorted, and transported to storage the approximate ton of winter squash, Linsey felt both pleased and exhausted, satisfied with a productive day even as the background anxiety of the city—though quiet throughout the day, so far as she knew—still gnawed at her. She hugged Katherine as they stood at the edge of the field. "Tell Jesse to be safe and that I hope he heals up soon, okay?"

"I will."

"And give your father my regards. And you . . . sleep, and be safe. Okay?"

She nodded. "Okay." They both stood silent a moment and then Katherine asked again, "What do you think will happen tonight?"

"Hopefully nothing," she said. "I haven't heard any sirens today."

"I checked a bit ago—no news."

"Good."

Katherine stared at her another long moment. "Part of me wants to be out there. For Jesse, for my dad . . . for everyone who keeps being stomped on."

"I know," Linsey said. "But I want you here tomorrow, too. This also helps. Feeding people helps. We need all of this."

Katherine nodded. "Yeah," she said, her voice trailing and uncertain, eyes echoing her tone. Then she shrugged. "I *will* be here tomorrow."

"Good."

She suddenly laughed, though tinged with sadness. "This is the way I like being tired. Not last night—not the worry. Just this, tired physically, worn out from work."

"I know," Linsey said. "Me too."

Katherine stared out at the field a moment, at the now-broken squash plants scattered and heaped across the beds. "Yeah. Okay. I'll see you tomorrow." Then she looped on her backpack, picked up her bike, gave Linsey a short wave and rode away, the tires crunching across the gravel as she heaved down on the pedals, working her way south and up the hill, heading, Linsey hoped, toward home.

Linsey took her time putting away her tools and equipment, checking out with Garrett at the Clubhouse and then walking the Sixth once more, bed by bed, to survey its state of affairs and plan the next couple days of work. She only half paid attention to the plants, though, her mind instead wandering into the realm of chaos and disintegration, injustice, the way the world kept grinding forward like an immense glacier and milling the land flat while sheering people from their bases: their homes and livelihoods, their communities and connections. The sun sank lower in the sky, deepening its blue toward darkness. Stars emerged, and then the pale gibbous moon, drifting southeast across the horizon and strengthening as the sun faded.

Tired, shaking herself from her pensive thoughts, Linsey wound her way out of the rows of crops, took one last look at the Sixth, and then set off for home at a slow pace, walking the same gravel path south out of Links as she had come in on. She worked her way into side residential streets, passing houses that varied wildly: a good many of them pleasant and in decent shape, with tended yards and new solar water heaters on south-facing roofs, buttressed often by the older solar photovoltaic panels that were legacies of the PV bubble of the early thirties; a good many others that were ramshackle and run down, in need of new paint jobs and their yards messier and chaotic, with small gardens picked over and turned ragged by the fall season, and older, makeshift solar water heaters on their roofs—or, as often as not, hastily rigged solar showers peaking out from side yards or around the back corner of the house. For a good while there, the neighborhood's housing stock had been steadily lurching downward in its upkeep and appearance, but once Helton and other private investment firms started in with force on their buying spree, the houses started getting new paint jobs, roofs repaired, new solar water heaters installed, and the yards cleaned up. This endeared them at first to the Council and to certain residents and neighborhood groups. But as the purchases continued, the evictions became more frequent, and the private security forces started enforcing those evictions as the Sheriff's pace slowed due to politics and public pushback, new fault lines started splitting and cleaving the city into warring factions. The flash protests and eviction response units organized by the fledgling No Home Without movement had become increasingly fractious and prone toward conflict with the security forces hired by Helton and other private firms. After the previous day's shooting, Linsey worried it would all spiral too far out of control.

And yet, the neighborhood felt quiet, even peaceful, as she walked it. No protests, no distant sirens, no commotion anywhere that she saw. She passed a few people sitting out on their porches—smoking, drinking, reading, sometimes just sitting and staring, perhaps appreciating the pleasant but chilly fall evening. Linsey nodded at some of them as she passed and they often did the same, giving a wave or calling out a greeting. As she turned a corner, she came upon a small, one story, trim olive green house with raised beds out front, the yard tidy. An older woman knelt at the edge of one of the raised beds in the evening twilight, faced out toward the street, digging deep into the soil as she pulled out potatoes one by one and added them to a large pile in the corner of the bed. The woman looked up and made eye contact with Linsey as she approached.

"Evening," Linsey said. "Looks like you have a nice bounty there."

The woman glanced at the pile of potatoes. She had grey hair, long and past her shoulders, and wore a ragged and patched flannel shirt. Her face was lined—handsome, but tired looking. Still, she smiled, even if it was wan. "Thank you," she said. "I always try to grow lots of potatoes for the winter."

"It's a good strategy. I do the same."

"You a gardener?" she asked.

"Yes. And a farmer. I have a plot over at Links."

"Oh," the woman said, and her smile twitched. "That's nice for you. I go to the market sometimes, though mostly I try to grow my own. Can't afford too much more than that. I don't know if I've seen you."

"It's a big market," Linsey said. "Easy for some of us to get lost in the shuffle." She nodded at the pile of potatoes. "You bring them in for winter?"

"Not normally all at once," the woman said. "But no use leaving 'em in the ground now. I gotta be out of here at the end of the month." The sky was growing darker now, fading into a glowing twilight behind the woman, a few more stars emerging. The dying light obscured the woman's face. "House got bought up." Her voice tightened. "I've lived her twenty years now, always got along great with my landlord. I kept the house up, she kept my rent affordable, she'd stop off sometimes and tell me how much she loved seeing these garden beds, knowing I was growing food here." She pulled out another potato, large and purple-skinned, and placed it on the pile. "I've always loved it here."

"I'm sorry," Linsey said. "Who bought the house? Someone moving into it?"

She laughed, sharp, and her voice rose. "Well, now, who do you think? Hell no, they aren't moving into it. They're raising the rent seventy percent and god knows I can't cover that with my social security. I tried to talk them into less, and they said no. I tried to ask them to wait, to at least give me a few months, and they said no." She smacked the edge of the bed with her open palm, then winced and muttered a curse under her breath. She quieted then, and a weariness entered her voice. "I told them I had put twenty years of my life into this place, and that I know I don't own it and I know they don't have to do a damn thing for me, but that I'm a good tenant they could make money off of if only they'd give me a fair deal. And they told me if I wasn't out in a month, they'd toss my ass on the curb." She leaned back, settling on her heels. "So I'm digging these damn potatoes so I at least have something to eat. I don't know where I'm going. I can't afford anything in this town no more."

The woman shook her head. Her house looked so pleasant behind her, its porch light on and casting a small glow upon a simple wicker chair and a small round table next to it, two potted plants on either side of the front door. Linsey wondered who would move in next—if they would tend to the garden beds the same or ignore them. It was amazing, in a city so riven with poverty after the economic crash of the late thirties, that Helton could still find so many people willing to pay such inflated rent prices to live in the up and coming neighborhoods. She oftened wondered where these people came from. Who paid their salaries?

"I'm sorry," Linsey said, wishing she had something better to say.

"Jesus," she said. "It's not your fault. It ain't you farmers screwing us over."

"I know, but—"

"Look," she said, her tone again sharp, "you got to watch out for yourself. We all got to watch out for ourselves. I'm sorry I rambled on you—it's really not your problem, it's mine. I've just been stewing on it out here, and you happened to stop and chat."

"I'm glad I stopped," she said.

"Don't be. You should be going on home and keeping your life together. Because believe me, we're all in the crosshairs—you too." She laughed. "Shit, you got to deal with the Council out there, don't you, there in Links?"

Linsey nodded. "There are a lot of politics."

"I bet."

"It's one of the more frustrating parts of growing there."

"I bet. I bet." The woman shook her head. "Look—you got someone at home?" She nodded again.

"What's his name? Her?"

"Brett."

"You love him?"

"Yes. He makes me a little crazy sometimes, but yes."

"My husband died ten years back. I still got memories of him back in that house." She paused, and her voice again grew thick. "That's one of the reasons I don't want to leave. I don't want to leave those memories here. I know that's dumb . . . I don't want to leave my neighbors, either, or my friends, or the cafe two blocks over where I have my Tuesday morning breakfast. I just want to keep my life." She picked up a potato, put it back down, then picked up another. The light just kept dying behind her, yet a few more stars scoured out into brightness by the gloom, just managing to slip past the city's background glow. "But maybe I just don't get to have it much longer, you know? But you got yours, you got your farm and you got your guy and you keep it, okay? Just go keep it."

"Okay," Linsey said, a sense of anxiety spreading, the sudden desire to flee. She almost took a step back but stopped herself. "Are you okay?" she asked, but she no longer knew if she wanted the answer.

"No, I'm not okay. But you got your life, so you go keep it."

"I'm sorry—"

"*Don't* be."

Linsey hesitated. "If I—"

"Oh, just go on home," the woman said, exasperated. "You got your life. You just got to get on home, okay? You don't know how long it's going to be there." Then she began picking up her potatoes, shoving them into a canvas bag lying at her feet, clumps of dirt raining down and her studiously looking away from Linsey until finally she turned and began walking away, trying not to walk too fast, trying to comprehend the ways in which she was wrong, the ways she was right, and unable to undersand which was which.

The apartment was dark and quiet when she arrived home. Unlocking the door and stepping into the solitude, she couldn't bring herself to be disappointed in or surprised by Brett's absence—what, really, had she expected?

She considered starting dinner but couldn't bring herself to be hungry, despite the day's work. Instead, she moved through the apartment, leaving it dark, and exited out the back door, into the south-facing lawn and their garden of deep dug beds heavy with a wide variety of vegetables. She always thought it somewhat silly that they kept such an extensive garden at home despite the fact that she farmed her own plot at Links, but Brett insisted that he enjoyed having something small and, in its agrarian ways, intimate for their own off-work attention. She had to admit that she did enjoy it, being able to come out to this small plot and weed and cultivate and tend to plants that didn't have to pay her living. There *was* a small relief in it.

To her surprise, a twelve foot section of bed was freshly flipped and dug, ready for the garlic to go in. He had worked at home today after all—at least for awhile. It brought her a small warmth, that fresh dirt in the now dark of night, the fact that he had carried through on crafting a piece of their home. But that warmth brought its own chill, as it left her realizing how little he seemed to carry through in that way of late—and how low the bar was for her to feel satisfaction.

Pulling her coat tight around her—the chill of the evening really was settling in now—she lowered herself down to the grass next to the garden, feeling its cold and damp through her jeans. She ran her hands down her legs and toward her feet, breathing out as her back stretched and ached, as her muscles whispered their approving disapproval. The clear sky yawned above her and she could feel her heat escaping into the earth, then imagined it escaping the earth up toward the heavens, wondering if the stress and frustrations riven through the city could do the same. She didn't want this tension anymore. She didn't want to have to ask herself constantly if she was doing enough or if she was missing a fight she owed the world or if putting food on tables was enough in its own right.

The night passed while she sat there thinking, growing colder, until she heard Brett come out the back door and down the steps, moving up behind her and then settling into the cold, wet grass next to her. His warmth touched her. She kept staring forward at the dug earth, waiting.

"I barely saw you out here," he said.

"Sorry," she said, then wanted to take it back. She was sick of saying sorry.

He shifted and tried to settle; sighed. "I'm sorry I'm late."

"Really?"

He paused. "Have you had dinner?"

"No."

"Do you want to?"

"I guess. I'm not that hungry."

He slipped a hand up from the small of her back, running over her coat. "Do you know what's happening out there?"

"What does that mean?" she asked, anger rising. "I know what happened in the field today. I know what happened to me—I know the work I did, the work Katherine did with me." She shifted, and his hand fell away. "Do you know what's happening *here*?" Finally she looked at him, and he held her gaze while his left hand ran back and forth through the grass, fingers on blades, dew collecting on his skin. "Okay," she said then, after a long moment of them evaluating each other. "Fine. What's happening out there?"

"There are plans for tomorrow. No Home Without—they're planning a major protest and march in Northeast and . . . I don't know, there are rumors they're going to take a house, maybe multiple houses that Helton has bought up."

"How do you know this?"

"I just came from a meeting. They're organizing."

"And you're, what? With them now? Are you a part of the group?"

"I may want to be. They have—" he stopped. She could imagine the look on her face, feel it, and even as she wished it could be different, she wanted him to see her anger. "They're trying to do good things."

"Who the hell isn't?"

"I'm not saying that."

"You're not saying what?"

She felt so cold now, all of it draining down into the earth and spreading through the soil below her. God, what she would give to be digging right now, to be weeding, to be cutting potatoes in the kitchen with Brett next to her, talking about plumbing. What she would give for dinner and conversation and sleep, all of it uncomplicated. What she would give for clear days and set schedules and a rhythm of subsistence she could count on—a place in the world clear to her.

"I thought you'd be happy I got the bed cleared," he said.

"Happier than I should be. It's hardly a thing."

The silence of him stewing next to her was as clear as anything. He stood, left, the back door slamming loud. She gave it a few moments, feeling the chill all around her and then standing, trying to bring warmth back into herself, not yet ready to be done. She followed him, but closed the back door quiet. The kitchen light was now on, the refrigerator door open, and he emerged from behind it holding a paper bag heavy with potatoes, staring fire at her.

"People are losing their homes," he said, dropping the potatoes on the counter.

She laughed. "Exactly. They're getting pulled right out from under them."

His face twisted with frustration. "What the hell does that mean?"

"It means—" she threw her hands up. "How the fuck do you think I feel?"

"About *what*?" he demanded.

"About losing this!" she yelled, flinging her hands out. "About losing you, us, this life that we've been building together—to all of this goddamn fury. I feel like I'm losing *my* home! You're gone, and detached, and ready to go fight in the streets while I'm trying to hold all this together and do something that matters, to feed people, to grow some goddamn food for people in this town! And it's like it's not enough, that I'm not doing enough for not going out in the streets and fighting because I'm too busy doing the *work*!" She lowered her voice, trying to will herself back to a steadiness, but her voice came out cold anyway. "The way you look at me sometimes."

His voice was a challenge. "How do I look at you?"

"Like I'm not good enough for you."

He said nothing. She stared at him. He struggled—she could see it, his face betraying everything, but in no clear ways. Slowly, though, the anger broke apart into sadness, into haunted frustration and confusion. Then he came to her and hugged her, his face pressed into her hair and hers into his shoulder..

"I'm sorry," he whispered.

"I am, too," she said.

"Can we try this again?" he asked.

She hesitated. "It feels like I'm going to lose everything."

"You aren't," he said.

"I might."

"No."

"I might," she said, and they both stood silent.

She broke away from him and moved into the bedroom, lying down on the bed and suddenly feeling exhausted, worn away by everything. Brett followed and stood before her a moment, looking down at her, his face a mix of worry and apprehension, misery, broken of all its anger. She looked at him for what felt like such a long time. Finally he crawled into the bed next to her. She turned and he pressed himself up against her back, slipping an arm around her and pressing his hand light against her stomach. They stayed like that, breathing together, finding the rhythm between them they had found so many times before but that somehow, someway, could still go missing so easily, sometimes in the least expected ways.

"I want to keep us," she whispered.

He kissed her, light, on the back of her neck. "Me too."

She knew that more needed to be said—that they were not fine, not settled yet—but she closed her eyes as the exhaustion spread throughout her. With the quiet and the steady rhythm of breath, Brett's warmth behind her, his light touch on her stomach, she began to slip into the in-between of sleep and wake, small voices slipping out of the ether to reveal conversations from some other realm. She could feel the link between her and Brett: tentative but strong, something passing back and forth in their breathing—no longer synced but interplayed, inhalations and exhalations playing off each other. Was she taking him in? Was he her? Above, she saw them both lying on the bed and could see thin tendrils of each others' breath passing back and forth between them—some attempt to infuse the other with their inner knowledge, with all their internal struggles and doubts, their deep fears. She could taste him and almost knew, then, everything he wanted, all the good and terrible desires he had, his frustration and deep love and—

Sirens erupted then, loud and not far away, a police car intent on some destination, shattering her out of her proto-sleep and view from above. She twitched and jerked even as Brett did the same, turning away from her, his hand gone from her stomach, their breaths lost in the shock. A moment later, another siren broke out at a different pitch—*Ambulance?* Linsey wondered, still struggling to bring herself back to the woken world—farther away but also close. Brett sat up. The sirens were so loud, insistent—and then a slammed door, someone yelling, close by. Linsey brought herself up now, too, rising up on an elbow and turning to look over at Brett. "What's happening?" More shouting came from outside, maybe in the street, maybe somewhere else—she couldn't tell. "Brett?" she said.

He turned to her even as he started to swing his legs out from the bed. "What's happening out there?" he asked.

"I don't know," she said.

He started to stand, but she grabbed his arm and pulled him toward her. "Brett," she said again, but he was looking now at the bedroom door, toward the living room and front door beyond—the outside world, screaming for attention. "Lay here with me," she said.

He paused and looked back at her. "There's something going on out there."

"I know. There always is." She leaned over and looped her arm around him, pushing her hand against his stomach, remembering vaguely the tendrils of breath slipping back and forth between them. "Look, tomorrow we can go back out there. But right now . . ."

"Do you think everyone's alright out there?"

"No," she said. "They never are."

"I should check."

She tugged on him, pressed deeper into his stomach, risked hurting him. Her voice came out slow and tight, forceful, each word enunciated. "Lay with me."

"Linsey," he said.

"Tonight, babe," she said. "You're here tonight, okay? Tomorrow you can go back out there, we both will. But tonight I need you here, in our home, with me. *Ignore* it. You're not going to fix it." He kept staring at the bedroom doorway, out toward the rest of the world. She put her hand on his shoulder and tried to will him to see again their home together—to remember what they already had. "They are not okay out there, but we're also not okay in here. You don't know what you can do out there—I don't either—but you're needed *here*. *I* know what you can do *here*. Do you even see it?"

She thought he wouldn't respond, that he wouldn't stay, and she was already trying to imagine what it would be after, once he left and she would be forced to make a decision. But after a long moment, he turned away from the door and lay back down on the bed, facing her. He watched her with an expression too conflicted for her to fully understand—he probably couldn't, either—but with a softness that relieved her. He touched the back of her neck. The sirens continued outside, still so loud and insistent, still so close. She closed her eyes, opened them, stared into his, and then tried to see past him, back to his breath. Tried to see it coming out of him and into her. Tried to see their shared connection, all the things that bound her to him and him to her. And she wanted only to reach toward it, to test its strength, and to see if it might still be there in the future no matter what happened outside: no matter how many sirens screamed, how many people felt their lives slipping out from beneath them, and how many reached out for something to grab onto, threatening to unravel everything that still stood beneath the weight of their shared desperation.

REVIEWS

AMERICA IN AUTUMN

Little, Big
Bantam Books, 1981

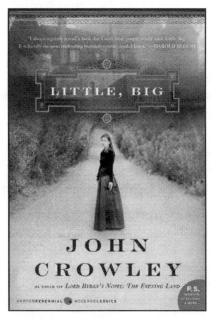

&

Beasts
Doubleday, 1976

Engine Summer
Bantam Books, 1979

all written by
John Crowley

IT'S COMMON FOR WORKS of deindustrial science fiction to focus on the contrast between the vanished world of modern industrial society and whatever imagined future the author wants to portray. That's certainly an option, but it's not the only option. Just as many stories in other flavors of science fiction use their imagined futures purely as a background against which the plot unfolds, without making the whole tale depend on a contrast with the present, it's equally possible to tell a tale placed in a deindustrial setting that isn't primarily about the decline, fall, and aftermath of our civilization. Two of the three novels I'll be discussing this time fall into this latter category; the third is very much about the contrast between our world and the deindustrial future—and though none of the stories are linked, all three take place in the northeastern United States at various points along a shared trajectory of decline.

John Crowley, their author, is one of the most consistently original authors of fantasy fiction writing today—one of the few who's stayed entirely away from the collection of tropes that was first assembled by J.R.R. Tolkien and has been overworked so relentlessly and unimaginatively since his time. Crowley is also one of the most literary authors in the genre, and his writing has more in common with Latin American magic realism than it does with your common and garden variety fantasy novel. Thus, for example, none of the three books discussed here has the sort of straight-ahead linear plot that's standard in so much modern science fiction and fantasy, with a hero or heroine pursuing some kind of goal in the teeth of opposing forces. Subtler and more lyrical, they reach their destinations by unexpected routes.

For all that Crowley's later reputation has centered on fantasy, *Beasts* is a straightforward work of science fiction set some decades into the notional future. Within living memory, civil wars tore the United States into a patchwork of quarrelling Autonomies. What remains of the federal government is trying to force a reunification, and it has the powerful backing of the Union for Social Engineering (USE), an organization of ruthless and dogmatic technocrats who want to impose their own ideas of a rationalist Utopia on the nation and the world. "Cropheaded, ill-dressed, intent," Crowley has one character call them, and another reflects on their use of opaque technical cant: "social erg-quotients and a holocompetent act-field and the rest of it." I knew such men in the

early 1980s, on the computer- and technology-obsessed end of the sustainability movement that was in the process of guttering out just then.

One wild card in play is that the former United States is not just inhabited by human beings. Genetic engineers in previous decades had mingled human and animal cells. (Crowley is here riffing off the earliest forms of genetic engineering, the ones known or imagined in the 1970s, so this was a matter of mashing cells together and seeing what happened, not of the precise gene splicing we have now.) Most of the attempted fusions didn't have viable results, but by some twist of chromosomal chance, human and lion cells produced a new species that bred true. Leos, as the resulting hybrids are called, have a small but self-sustaining population in the former United States. There is also one other hybrid, the sole member of its species: a fox-human who goes by the name Reynard. All such hybrids are loathed by USE, which sees them as an impediment to Man's conquest of nature.

The stark autumnal landscape of the eastern seaboard of post-U.S. North America provides the scenery against which the resulting conflicts play out. Across that backdrop move a skillfully mismatched set of characters—the naturalist and falconer Loren Casaubon; Painter the leo, and Cassie, the indentured servant who becomes his lover; Sten and Mika Gregorius, the children of the assassinated Director of the Northern Autonomy; the wildlife photographer Meric Landseer; a dog named Sweets, who has awakened to humanlike intelligence as a result of medical experimentation; a peregrine falcon known only as Hawk; and Reynard the fox-man, adept political manipulator, who plays Merlin's role in setting the stage for the coming Arthur.

Each of these characters has his or her own story, and each of those stories weaves back and forth across the landscape of the novel, encountering the others at various points and tangling with the broader sequence of events as federal officials and USE operatives struggle with the Autonomies, the leos, and others. Only in the final pages of the book do all the characters arrive in a single place, and the results of that encounter—typically, for Crowley—are implied rather than displayed. Indirect and evasive as the story seems at first glance, it's a satisfying read.

Engine Summer is a very different book, and it's set at an equally different point in the long curve of decline and fall. It's the first-person story, artlessly told, of a young man named Rush that Speaks, a member of the truthful speakers who dwell in Little Belaire, a ramshackle half-town, half-dwelling in the nameless wooded landscape that emerged long after the twilight years of the United States of America.

The truthful speakers don't remember that name. To them, the half-remembered time before theirs was a world of angels, and the Storm that ended the angels' world stands like a shadow near the beginning of all tales. Only the Long League of women and a plethora of half-understood technologies, some of which still function, survive from before that event. Accounts of the Storm itself are vague, scattered with dim memories of the people who fought against the angels and the vast desperate dreams of the angels themselves in their last days, when they hoped to build cities in the sky and to live forever, or almost.

It was after the Storm that the stories began: the time when the truthful speakers wandered, an age of saints and wonders, before the founding of Little Belaire. The saints—St. Andy and St. Bea, Great St. Roy and Little St. Roy, and the rest of them—form the texture of the past that Rush that Speaks knows as he grows up. His present is defined by Little Belaire, sprawling, shapeless, and constantly changing, with temporary walls rising here and being taken down there, and Path winding through all of it, understood only by those who walk it. The stories he hears, though, whisper of a lost treasure of the angels, and when the girl he loves leaves Little Belaire to go with the Society of Dr. Boots' List, he leaves as well, partly hoping to follow her, partly in search of the lost secrets of the angel's world.

It would be too much of a spoiler to describe what Rush that Speaks encounters and how he changes and learns, much less what the treasure of the angels' world is that he finds and the exceedingly strange way that he finds it. What deserves discussion here is the way that the world of *Engine Summer* is built out of accidental repurposings, reimaginings, and misunderstandings of our world. The book's title is a good starting place. In the northeastern United States, "Indian summer," almost always pronounced "Injun summer," is a spell of warm clear weather that comes after the beginning of autumn. In the mouths of the truthful speakers in Rush that Speaks' time, that's morphed into "engine summer"—a mordant reminder that in their time, the age of engines is as far in their past as the age of Indian wars is in ours.

The same sort of haphazard repurposing runs all through *Engine Summer*, with results as instructive as they are elegant. The gossips who serve as priestesses, teachers, and oracles to the truthful speakers, for example, base much of their wisdom on an ancient artifact, a set of glass slides called the Filing System. Back in the angels' time, that was the Condensed Filing System for Wasser-Dozier Multiparametric Parasocietal Personality Inventories, Ninth Edition, and therapists apparently used it for scoring tests used in personality studies. To the gossips, it's a tool for divination; two or three or four slides stacked together and looked through make patterns that reveal the secrets of the

present and the future. And so it goes, spiraling outward through a future world in which the fabric of meanings our time has woven together out of its ideas and its artifacts has been picked to pieces and knotted together into a completely different pattern.

What makes all this work so well in the context of the story is the way that Rush that Speaks, as he tells his story, treats every detail as perfectly normal and obvious, the ordinary background of an ordinary life, if you happen to be a truthful speaker raised in Little Belaire with a head full of stories about saints and angels. It's a subtle trick: by pushing those details into the background, Crowley forces the reader to notice them, and to experience the dizzying cultural and conceptual distance separating the world of Rush that Speaks from our world.

Little, Big, finally, is a project on a much grander scale than the two books already discussed, a huge and sprawling novel that covers more than a century in time, from the late nineteenth century to sometime in our near future. It's also an example of that comparative rarity, a work of deindustrial fantasy that really works. Yes, there is such a genre, mostly made up of stories in which the collapse of industrial society leads by some collection of gimmicks to the reappearance of elves, wizards, dragons, magic swords, and the rest of the stage properties of generic post-Tolkien fantasy fiction. (Those readers who know their way around late twentieth century Tolkienesque kitsch may recall that Terry Brooks' novel *The Sword of Shannara* and Ralph Bakshi's movie *Wizards*, two early and unimpressive examples of the type, were both rather implausibly set in a post-nuclear holocaust future.)

That's not what John Crowley did, though, not by a long shot. *Little, Big* is a fantasy novel, in that fairies and magic are important to the story, but the fairies are not generic post-Tolkien elves, and the magic is nothing you'll find in the pages of your average fantasy novel. The fairies, rather, are those elusive beings found in classic fairy tales, and the magic is based on a range of genuine occult traditions, ranging from the high magic of the Renaissance to African-diaspora traditions of the kind you'll encounter in urban botanicas today. There's no generic Dark Lord in *Little, Big*, nor a magic McGuffin that has to be destroyed or saved or found or lost or what have you, in order to defeat the Dark Lord and keep the world from changing. Quite the contrary, the villain of the piece is a figure about as far from a generic Dark Lord as you care to imagine; there's a magic McGuffin of sorts, a deck of cards, but its functions as a plot engine are far more subtle, multiple, and ultimately terrifying than anything you'll find in your common or garden variety fantasy novel; and by the end of the tale the characters, the United States, and the world have all changed irrevocably into new things, rich and strange.

The tale begins as a young man named Evan "Smoky" Barnable leaves New York City on foot, heading for a place in upstate New York named Edgewood, where he will marry. His bride-to-be Alice Drinkwater and her family live there; they and the other families of the area are descended from a colony of Theosophists who gathered there in the late nineteenth century, around a visionary named Violet Bramble who could speak with fairies. Smoky arrives, marries Alice, and becomes part of the subtle magic of the Edgewood community—for the lines of communication with the fairies remain open, focusing on the strange and sprawling Drinkwater house and on an ancient deck of cards Violet Bramble brought with her from England.

Time passes, children are born, the world outside Edgewood begins to stumble down a familiar arc of decline. Twenty-five years after Smoky's journey, his son Auberon makes the same trip in reverse, arriving in a rundown, impoverished, chaotic New York City where urban farms are springing up in the middle of old residential blocks. He hopes to find his fortune in the city; what he finds instead is a long strange journey through love, loss, magic, and transformation, sending him like a weaver's shuttle back and forth through the destiny of Edgewood and its families—and also through the destiny of the United States of America.

"A touchy, wilful, aging republic suffering in the more or less permanent grip of social and economic depression"—that's the America of *Little, Big*. Its official government is a sideshow; the real power is held by an inner circle of bankers, board chairmen, bureaucrats and retired generals, comprising an organization whose name is one of the minor delights of the story and will be left to the reader to discover. Advising them from time to time, at their request, is the elegant figure of Ariel Hawksquill, the greatest mage of that age of the world, whose occult powers are rooted in the ancient Art of Memory.

Meanwhile, far from New York City, traveling from speaking gig to speaking gig in a succession of states whose names begin with I, is Russell Eigenblick, the Lecturer, a charismatic demagogue who has a secret name. Ariel Hawksquill will learn Eigenblick's secret and ally with him as he rises to absolute power, and she will be caught up in a strange fashion in his sudden and eerie fall—and that fall will also bring about the dissolution of the United States in civil war and forced migration, echoing the core historical themes of *Beasts* and *Engine Summer*. That's the background against which Smoky and Alice, their son Auberon, his lover Sylvie, and a galaxy of other characters finish tracing out the intricate destiny set in motion long before by Violet Bramble and the fairies who communicated with her.

All in all, *Little, Big* is a major work of fantasy—it richly deserved the World Fantasy Award it won—and it's also an extraordinary work of deindustrial fiction. More generally, all three of Crowley's deindustrial novels have much to offer the reader and writer of our genre.

———————

In future issues of *Into the Ruins*, I plan on continuing this column and surveying the desolate but enticing landscapes portrayed by past authors of deindustrial SF. While I have a good many books already lined up to review, there's doubtless no shortage of stories of that kind that I haven't read or don't remember. If you have favorites you'd like to propose for review, or for that matter really dreadful examples of the species, by all means drop me a note c/o *Into the Ruins* at joel@intotheruins.com, or by mail at:

Figuration Press
3515 SE Clinton Street
Portland, OR 97202

Many thanks!

The Mandibles:
A Family, 2029-2047

by Lionel Shriver

Harper, 2016

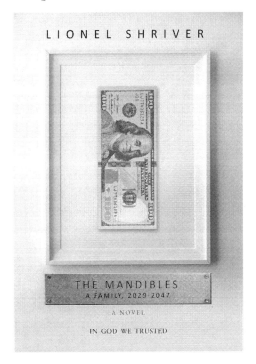

THE MANDIBLES IS THE MOST curious of books because it's essentially a doomerseque tale of economic Armageddon packaged up as respectable contemporary literature.

Lionel Shriver, known for her incisive and unflinching takes on contemporary American life, has previously penned novels whose subject matter includes high school mass shootings, the obesity epidemic and the failings of the healthcare system. In *The Mandibles*, Shriver turns her merciless gaze to the world of economics and delivers a dystopian near-future scenario so plausible that there have been reports of people stockpiling food and supplies the moment after they have turned the last page.

The story concerns the eponymous family, spread out over four generations and—generally speaking—enjoying to differing degrees the fruits of living in the world's richest economy. All that changes when the dollar loses its reserve currency status and a cascading series of crises bear down upon the country as a result. The economic ruination kicks off in the year 2029—symbolically, a century after the Great Depression—when a new reserve currency is launched jointly by Russia and China.

The 99-year-old patriarchal head of the family, Douglas, is sitting on the family fortune amassed from the production of diesel engines in the twentieth century. His children—themselves in late middle age—await their inheritance with some degree of impatience, although, frustratingly, Douglas shows no signs of shuffling off his mortal coil and still enjoys a brisk game of tennis. A generation further down and we have Florence, just about holding things together working at a homeless shelter in New York City and living in an apartment with her Mexican partner and precocious teenage son Willing. For Florence and her family, the economic hard times have already hit some years ago, meaning every drop of water is rationed and meals are basic. Perhaps because of this, Willing has developed an obsession with economics and finance and is fully aware of the precarious state of the nation.

In sharp contrast to her sister Florence, Avery lives in a "smart" apartment in Washington DC with her husband Lowell, a tenured economics professor of a neoliberal Keynesian persuasion. They have two sons named after search engines—Goog and Bing—and their comfortable lives revolve around dinner parties, book launches and trying to stop their dysfunctional intelligent apartment from killing them. Lowell, with his techno-progressive mindset, comes across as the epitome of smug neoliberalism and is predictably clueless about the approaching calamity.

Florence and Avery have an aunt, too: a one-hit novelist who has spent the last few decades living in Paris but returns to the U.S. when things get rough for Americans abroad. And lurking in the background of the story is their doomer brother Jarred, who tries to warn the family of what is coming and bugs out to a farm in upstate New York to grow his own food. Predictably, his affluent sister Avery and her husband mock Jarred, although he returns much later in the story to play a prominent role in their salvation.

When the economic crisis hits, the family find themselves penniless more or less overnight. Douglas, for all his supposed investment wisdom, loses the paper money his offspring had for so long had their eyes on. The plush residential nursing home he resides in teeters on the edge of bankruptcy as normal everyday life is thrown into reverse gear. We get to follow the family members as they deal with the loss of their jobs, their homes and their prestige, eventually seeing them all end up jammed together in the long-suffering Florence's tiny New York apartment.

There are two things you should know about *The Mandibles*. The first is that it has a somewhat lugubrious start. There's a very good reason for this. Lionel Shriver has clearly done her homework, immersing herself in the opaque and complex world of practical and theoretical economics, and she wants to make the story as plausible as can be. This means there are quite a few pages of talk about reserve currency statuses, GDP-to-debt ratio spreads, derivatives markets and all the rest of it. As a reformed economics junkie I can confirm that she isn't just making it up, but the good news is that if this sort of thing bores you it is possible to skip over some of the longer dinner party conversations without any loss of narrative clarity. All you need to know is that America becomes poor. All of a sudden. And nobody knows how to fix it.

Secondly, be aware that this is a satire. Dark, dark satire. The humour in this story is so inky black it oozes off the page like bituminous crude oil. In fact, so dry is the drollery the casual reader might not even be aware of it—although I imagine Shriver wrote the entire book with an impish smirk playing on her lips. Thus we have the economics professor so marinated in the infallibility of his own economic theory that even as his own life disintegrates around him he insists that it can't be happening because the models don't allow for it. In Shriver's story, everything is metaphor—even the name of the family "Mandible," who are chewed up and spat out by an economic system they thought they could rely on. On the front cover of the book there's a picture of a one hundred dollar bill, and underneath the words "In God We Trusted."

The family, shoved together through circumstance, eventually even lose the roof over their heads and are forced on a modern-day *Grapes of Wrath* type trek to Jarred's doomstead (Jared Diamond—the author of *Collapse?*). Awful things happen to them en route, but then the action moves forwards into the year 2047 for the next act—and just when you thought the story couldn't get much darker . . . it does. Order has been restored to a shattered America, but it has come at a price that becomes horrifyingly clear as the novel draws to its conclusion, revealing a big twist at the end which explains a thing or two.

All in all I found *The Mandibles* hugely enjoyable. What could well have been a dry and depressing story is told with a kind of warm wit that speaks of the battle of the human spirit against physical adversity and soul

crushing bureaucracy. It's probably worth reading just for the gallows humour; at one point I was so convulsed with laughter my daughter rushed into the room thinking I was having some kind of seizure. And for all the human flaws inherent in the characters, none are portrayed without sympathy—and that makes *The Mandibles* a very compassionate tale.

—*Jason Heppenstall*
22billionenergyslaves.blogspot.com

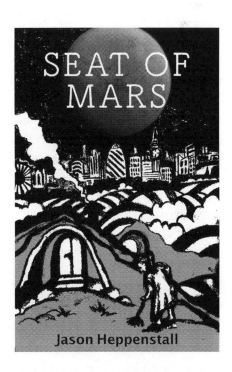

Don't miss Jason Heppenstall's new deindustrial science fiction novel, *Seat of Mars*, published by Club Orlov Press.

Learn more at
cluborlovpress.blogspot.com

Renew Your Subscription Now!

It's time to renew your subscription! Okay, for a few of you, it isn't—but the majority of you have subscriptions running from the first issue through the fourth. And since this is the fourth issue, that means many subscriptions just expired.

This project has proven more successful than I thought likely. I didn't expect it to fail, mind you, but I didn't necessarily expect this level of interest, enthusiasm, and excitement. It's due to all of you subscribers that I have been able to make this project happen. It's also why I've been able to increase the rate I pay our contributing authors each issue. While I sell issues beyond the subscriber base, you are the guaranteed income that allows me to financially plan for the future of this project, set my author payment rates, and otherwise strategize about the magazine's direction going forward, as well as how much time I can afford to dedicate to this project.

Therefore, I ask that, if you enjoy *Into the Ruins* and the stories within, if you want this project to continue into another year and to grow, please renew your subscription now. The sooner the better. Knowing my subscriber base allows me to better plan for the fifth issue, set my pay rates, and otherwise move forward in a confident manner.

To renew your subscription now, please mail a check or money order made out to Figuration Press for $39 (if you're in the U.S.) to:

Figuration Press
c/o Joel Caris
3515 SE Clinton Street
Portland, OR 97202

or to pay by credit card or renew an international subscription, visit:

intotheruins.com/renew

68287894R00064

Made in the USA
Charleston, SC
07 March 2017